25 Old Fashioned English Stories

*****

Jessie Booth

25 Old Fashioned English Stories

These short stories were penned over a period of more than forty years by an old fashioned hand. You'll find only the occasional mention of a computer or cell phone in the most recent stories. One story is even set in Victorian England. You will also find stories involving visitors from other planets, young love, murder, a young woman who has a brush with death and gets a whole new lease on life, visits from the afterlife, an elderly gentleman who thwarts would be robbers…. and many more.

The murders are subtly diabolical, the love stories sweet, the philosophical stories thoughtful and the alien tales unusual.

Individual Story Descriptions:

1. Poor Old Joe

Everyone is sick of 'Poor Old Joe' and they ensure he gets exactly what he deserves.

2. Linda's Box

A beach find proves perilous to a young woman whose husband is away.

3. Just Joking

The joke is on you if you think you can toy with this feisty lady and survive.

4. Laura's Love

A chocoholic gets much more than she ever bargained for when she begins dating a young man who understands her addiction.

5. Smoke Screen

When it comes to saving her grandson, Annie is not the easy mark her blackmailer expects.

6. In Between

A near death experience inspires an unmotivated young woman to change her lacklustre ways.

7. A Lady of Merit

A sweet and gentle love story involving Lady, a lovable dog and the humans who adore her.

8. And So, To Bed

A practical joking brother finds that the joke is on him.

9. Mr. Bates

A widower enjoys his solitude and a very singular hobby, until burglars interrupt his quiet world and get the surprise of their lives.

10. Strange Happenings

A young reporter is sent to investigate strange happenings in a small quiet village and discovers a whole lot more than he bargains for.

11. Time Goes By

A young childless couple think they have their future mapped out until a young boy warms their hearts.

12. One Special Day

A little girl has a special day out and meets some tiny out of this world new friends.

(This is a short story to read to children)

13. Take a Chance

A young woman stuck in a repetitive factory job takes a

vi

chance on a new line of work which leads to a new opportunity in her personal life.

14. One by Another

A petulant young woman marches out of a village dance and has a life changing experience.

15. Grey Day

A quiet elderly gentleman gives would-be robbers exactly what they deserve, and it's the last thing they expect.

16. So Ordinary

A lonely widow finds new friends thanks to a persistent furry visitor.

17. The Joker

The family joker and the new man in a young woman's life discover they have something in common.

18. Solly

An alien observer is sent to file a report on human behaviour and he is not impressed.

19. Lucky Seven

The seventh child of a seventh child is told that she should have special powers, but is that a gift or a curse?

20. Temperate Feeling

A young woman visits a botanic garden built on the site of

a former hospital and experiences some very unusual sensations and an otherworldly message.

21. Spring Clean

A husband's frustration with his constantly cleaning wife is quickly abated with a view of the other side of the coin.

22. Kidnapped

A small boy in Victorian England faces hardship and hunger before finding happiness.

23. Autumn Years

A couple in their autumn years discover that worrying about the future is unnecessary.

24. The Last Waltz

A tired lady enjoys a quiet day in the park and a last waltz with a gentle stranger.

25. Comes the End

Visitors from another planet infiltrate Earth, but soon discover that they are not the most powerful beings in the universe after all.

Table of Contents

Poor Old Joe

Everyone is sick of 'Poor Old Joe' and they ensure he gets exactly what he deserves.

Dear God, here he comes again! The neighbours would all be complaining tomorrow, that song was a nightmare! He always came rolling up the street drunk singing the same song. *'Poor old Joe, out in the snow, nowhere to shelter and nowhere to go'*. It didn't matter what time of year it was, the same words always rang out for everyone to hear. She opened the door as he came closer and he stumbled over the step, "Nobody loves me," he wept as he almost fell into the room.

Audrey helped him into an armchair and again he began singing, *'Poor old Joe'*. She hastily grabbed hold of his boots knowing he would stop if she began undressing him. "Leave me alone, woman! Can't a man sing in his own house?" he grumbled.

"Joe, you must be tired, I only want you to go and have a rest now," she soothed.

He grunted and fell back into the chair. "I want my supper first, and no rubbish either." Audrey got up from her knees and went to the kitchen where she pretended to prepare food for her husband. After a few minutes she peered around the door, sure enough, as usual Joe was fast asleep. It was always the same, every time he had enough money for a drink he was off to the Dark Horse and Groom, and always came home in this state. By experience Audrey had learnt to coax him into sleep, he would wake up grumpy and complaining but that was better than making him angry and being beaten, or getting him a meal only for him to waste it. There was little enough money without any being wasted on good food that had to be thrown away.

The dreams she'd had as a young girl of being happily married to the handsome Joseph had quickly disappeared as reality set in. Six babies, little money, and Joe's drinking had soon chased away her hopes of a loving husband and a nice home. The neighbours pitied her, she knew that, but Joe scorned them all, he didn't care for anyone but his drinking cronies.

She had tried pleading, reasoning, but nothing worked, a beating was all she got for her trouble. So now she had decided on new tactics because she wasn't finished yet, no, not by a long shot.

Tonight must be the night. She wanted better for her children than a life of fear and going without, and at thirty-six she was still young and reasonably attractive herself. Two hours had gone by when she looked at her husband again. Joe was laid back in the armchair, his mouth wide open. She covered him with a blanket and putting on her coat went outside. All the terrace houses on her street were now in darkness, well, not surprising as it was one-thirty in the morning. Going down to the end of the street, Audrey crossed the road.

It was three in the morning when she returned and went back into her home, stepping quietly over Joe's outstretched legs she climbed the stairs and quickly got ready for bed.

It was a cry from her twelve year old son Stephen that roused her; she jumped up and hurried downstairs. Joe was still in the chair but his eyes were open and staring. Quickly Audrey checked, yes, Joe was dead. She sent Stephen for a neighbour and ushered the other children into the front room.

The neighbours were very kind, they soon had everything under control, the body was gone and Audrey sat with a cup of tea. There were murmurs of sympathy for a young widow with six children, and hushed whispers of how she would be better off without him really anyway.

The inquest decided that Joe had died of alcohol poisoning; everyone knew his reputation so no one was surprised by the verdict.

Six months later Audrey married Tim Foster, a widower who lived on the next street with his two children. Everyone was pleased for them both and agreed it was a good match.

They had been married for three months and were living in the terraced house that had been Joe's and Audrey's, it had three double bedrooms and an attic room, and with eight children between them, made more sense than Tim's two up two down home. Audrey sighed with contentment, "I'm so happy, Tim, our children get on well and I'm so glad you don't drink. That night was awful, wasn't it!" She shuddered at the memory.

Tim patted her hand. "Don't you worry now, it's all over.

4

He deserved what he got."

"But waking him up and getting him to drink more and more beer and lacing it with spirits wasn't easy, I thought he would pass out before I could get him to swallow enough! Then when he did collapse, putting a cushion over his face was scary; I daren't press too hard in case I left any marks. I just had to come to you for comfort before going to bed."

"Well, it worked and we are alright, aren't we?" said Tim.

Suddenly his eyes opened wide, his jaw dropped and Audrey sprang to her feet with a shriek. *"Poor old Joe, out in the snow, nowhere to shelter and nowhere to go"*. The words drifted around them as they clutched each other.

Upstairs, Danny, Tim's youngest who was ten, was listening in puzzlement as his tape recorder played the song, then he remembered. It was an old tape he'd been practicing with months ago at the bottom of the street, trying to pick up sounds at night. Better not to let his dad know about it, he had crept out late that night and should have been in bed. He quickly switched off his machine and settled down to sleep.

The End

Linda's Box

A beach find proves perilous to a young woman whose husband is away.

As she strolled along the beach, Linda cast her eyes upwards, what movement was it that she had seen? The towering cliff showed nothing but seagulls wheeling about. She shook her head *I must stop imagining I can see things when I don't.*

The sea lapped in gently; soon she must turn and go back before the tide sent water to the bottom of the cliffs. It was so peaceful here, in the distance a couple was walking with a dog which kept running joyfully into the water's edge. This was a quiet beach and in November few people came along. Surprisingly the sun shone and even in the cold air it was good to be out. Well wrapped and warm, this was the perfect spot for a winter walk. Finally with regret she turned and began to go back toward the slope that led up from the beach.

As she did so, she saw a green package floating in the shallows. Without a second thought she waited until the waves slid back and picked it up before the water came in again. It was flat, about two feet long, and the green covering was obviously waterproof. So far on this beach in winter she had found only numerous odd shoes, flip-flops, plastic bottles, a penknife, and lots of rubbish. Should she throw it in the bin or not?

Well, as she had it she might as well take it home with her and see what it was. When Linda reached her cottage which was set back from the cliffs, she put the package down in the kitchen, and then took off her coat and boots before switching on the kettle for a hot drink.

She locked her door, drew the curtains and then stood looking at the package. Her husband Jon worked away from home and would not be back for another week, so she was all alone with her cat Timmy. First she made a cup of coffee, and then as Timmy was rubbing around her legs she fed him, talking to him as she did so.

Settling down at the kitchen table she began to unwrap the package very slowly, for it had now occurred to her it might be something not very nice. As the wrapping came away she saw it was a box about twelve inches square. There was a lot of wrapping before she came to the box itself, but there seemed nothing remarkable about it at all. It was shiny and black with no marks of any kind, and no obvious way into it either, yet it had some areas that were bumpy. A piece of modern art perhaps? Shrugging she set it aside.

The next day was bright and clear, so after breakfast having checked the tide was right, Linda decided to go for a walk along the beach again. As she wandered along her favourite beach there were one or two other folks about, but no one she knew. The usual rubbish had been washed ashore, but nothing of any interest to her. She took deep breaths of the clear air and was really enjoying the walk. Suddenly she was aware of a young man walking nearby; he smiled and wished her a good morning as he passed by. She gave no thought to this as so many people smiled and said a few words as they wandered along the beach.

Strangely, as Linda was preparing to go up the slope from the beach the young man was there again. "Well, hello, we meet again," he said.

Linda smiled and nodded but did not reply as she hurried away. It was the usual busy day from thereon, cleaning, baking and shopping. As she left the shops in the late afternoon she jumped as a voice at her elbow said. "What a small world it is, fancy seeing you again!"

"Yes, a very small world! Well, I must dash," Linda replied as she recognised the man from the beach. Quickly she hurried away, it was quite worrying really, why was he always at her heels?

When she got home she waited for Jon's call. She didn't tell him about the man—only about the funny box she had found. After a long chat they said goodnight. Jon had advised her to get rid of the box if it was nothing, or hand it in to the police if it appeared important.

Linda took out the box to have another look at it, if anything it looked more interesting than before. Then she remembered an old Chinese puzzle box her mother had, you had to go through a series of movements with it before it opened—pull out one piece, push in another and so on.

By now she was intrigued and began turning the box in her hands, pressing, easing, coaxing, and suddenly one piece on the side moved! She eased it over, then felt alongside it and pushed, another piece moved up, now she was getting excited. An hour later the box had moved in many ways, but there was no sign of being able to get into the middle of it. Perhaps it was simply a puzzle box and she wasn't meant to get into the heart of it? Tired, Linda got up and stretched. "Time for a warm drink!" she said tossing the box onto a chair—but it fell from the chair, hit the floor and sprang open.

"I must have been close to finding the heart of it when I threw it down after all," she mused aloud. Carefully she picked up the box and as she did so, realised something was in the centre of it. There was not a lot of room but the small space held a piece of velvet cloth, gently she eased it out and opened up the cloth. With a gasp she realised that it was a diamond, shining brightly, sparkling in the light of her overhead lamp and so beautiful. Linda sat down with a thump, gazing at it. Timmy purring at her feet brought her back to reality and made her realise where she was and what she had. Then she began to put a few thoughts together. The feeling someone was watching her from the cliff top, the young man who kept meeting her 'by accident'. Was he the one the box was intended for? Where was he now? Had he followed her home?

With her heart pounding, Linda quickly went from room to room checking all was secure. She had a habit of locking herself in while Jon was away, and how thankful she was that everywhere was secure. She picked up the box, carefully and slowly she wrapped the diamond and put it back inside. Jon had told her that he would be in a meeting tonight, and it would be a few more days before he returned home again, so what to do? Of course, she must ring the police. Putting the box down she went to the kitchen telephone. Having found the number for the local police station she dialled. Nothing. The line was dead. Again she tried with the same result.

Now she was scared, was it just that number? Quickly she tried another number but the phone was well and truly dead. What could she do? If she went out he might be waiting for her, how could she make contact with anyone outside? Then she heard it—a rustling near the window, there was no wind tonight so someone was brushing up against the shrubs beneath her living room window. Her mouth felt dry, and looking down at Timmy she realised he was no longer purring and his fur was standing up on his back as he gazed at the window. She backed out of the room taking the box with her and climbed the stairs to her bedroom, being careful to put on no lights. She peeped from the corner of the curtains which were drawn across the bedroom window, there was nothing to see outside, all seemed quiet and still. But she was sure someone was out there, her heart was pounding and she was trembling.

She felt a movement near her ankle and almost screamed,

12

then she felt Timmy's soft fur against her hand and realised he'd come to join her. There was a tapping on the door downstairs, which stopped suddenly, then after a short pause began again.

There was no way she was going to open the door, but how long could she ignore it? What would whoever was out there do? If only Jon was not so far away, and if only she had agreed to get a mobile phone! But it had not seemed necessary before now. Then she had an idea. Opening the window very gingerly she pushed Timmy out onto the roof. *Please let this work—please!* She closed the window as carefully as she had opened it. Now she was really frightened, and all alone without even the friendly presence of her cat.

The sounds from outside became more bold, a banging on the door, a rattling at the windows, the sound of footsteps on the path. Her neighbours, like herself, had quite large gardens and were not really close, so they would not hear anything. Then she heard the scrambling on the sloping roof under her bedroom window. As she sat curled up near the curtains, peeping under them, the windows began to shake but thankfully didn't open, the locks were holding, but what next? Linda moved away from the window and crept in darkness across the room. She went into the bathroom and put the chair she had in there under the door knob to hold the door against anyone coming in. The tiny bathroom window was impossible to get in or out of either.

Again there were sounds at the door downstairs; someone

was trying to get in. She sat on the floor in the darkness with the box and the diamond cupped in her hands. No lights were showing, but whoever it was would not go away. Then there was the sound of the door being hit, and a loud crack. *Oh no! They've broken the door down*, she thought.

There was a murmur of voices drawing near and footsteps coming up the stairs. She heard the click of each bedroom light going on and the rooms being searched, she knew the chair under the door handle would not hold them off for long. They came to a standstill at the door.

"Well, my sweet, if you had been more friendly and shown me what you picked up on the beach, this wouldn't have been necessary, would it?" a voice called. It was the young man from the beach, she recognised his voice.

"We know what you have there, it was meant for us so hand it over like a good girl," the voice continued.

If only she had told Jon about him! But she had not wanted to worry her husband. *So independent, Linda. Now what can you do?* she berated herself.

Well, she had tried one thing but with no result, so now she must face it when they broke the door down. Then she heard it, a rushing of feet, scuffles, shouting and lots of noise. The voice at the door was very gentle.

"Linda, are you in there? This is police officer Fraser, you

14

can open the door, we have all three of them." It was a woman's voice, she was safe! With trembling hands she moved the chair and opened the door. A police woman was there along with two male officers and her neighbours.

Soon they were all in the kitchen, her neighbour Mrs. Smith had made coffee for everyone. The box and diamond had been handed over and explanations given. Her neighbours, just as she had hoped, knew something was wrong when they saw Timmy, as he was never out at night. Timmy always made for their garden when he was out during the daytime, and mewed at their patio window until they let him in as they always had treats handy for him. But when he showed up after dark they knew something was wrong and a quick look outside had told them they were right. They had immediately phoned the police. She thanked all of them over and over again, and cuddled Timmy for being so clever. The police were sending someone to fix her door, but she and Timmy were spending the night with her neighbours.

The next morning the phone was reconnected and the house set to rights. Timmy was glad to be home after a night away. Jon had been called and was on his way home after the police explained what had happened.

There was a reward for the return of the diamond it seemed, and Linda knew a mobile phone was going to be a priority purchase. And a severe telling off by the police about bringing home mystery items found on the beach made Linda vow never again would she be tempted to bring things home. But the adventure had been quite something, and she had been allowed to keep the puzzle box. A memento of her adventure, something she would never forget.

The End

Just Joking

The joke is on you if you think you can toy with this feisty lady and survive.

Just joking? Freda remembered the times when Frank, her only son had put spiders in the bathtub, changed the sugar in the sugar dish for salt, put crispy dried leaves in her bed and holly in her pillow case—to name just a few of his favourite practical jokes. Oh yes, he always thought it was funny. And now the phone call to say he was coming home? She wished *that* was a joke.

Freda was sitting in her comfortable bungalow, thinking. She had been married to Sam for seventeen years when he had fallen under the wheels of a car ending his life. Not the driver's fault they said, as Sam had been well and truly drunk and must have tried to cross the road without looking.

Well, she wasn't really sorry; her marriage had gone from bad to worse since Sam had begun to drink heavily. After his father's death, Frank, who was sixteen had left home 'to go on the stage'. From then on she had heard very little from him, an occasional card or phone call, but they had not been very close, her son was too much like his father who Freda wanted to forget.

Working at one of the tills at the supermarket checkout Freda had met many regular customers, she didn't really like her job but it was a living. However, when Doug Rogers began taking an interest in her the job became important and she looked forward to his daily visits to the store.

They were soon going out together. Doug had lost his wife

through illness and they had comforted each other. He had no children and Freda considered she didn't really either since she so rarely heard from Frank.

Then after eight years of wedded bliss Doug had a heart attack, congenital the doctor said. It had been a weakness. Now at a relatively young age Freda was a widow again.

This time though, she did not have to work, she owned the bungalow outright and had a widow's pension, so she settled down after the first six months of widowhood quite comfortably. Now it was all going to be upset. Whatever did Frank want? She soon found out. He had met someone who knew her; they had told him she was a widow again but quite reasonably well-off.

So he had come to stay with his 'dear old mum'. Apart from the fact that she wasn't old, Freda soon began to resent his untidiness, the extra cooking and washing, and above all Frank's loud clothes and bad manners. She cringed when he walked past her neighbours' homes, and prayed he would not get into conversation with any of them.

After a month Freda knew it was time for him to go. The unfortunate thing was, he'd told her, "There's no need for me to work now that I have a wealthy mum." She was not wealthy, and already her savings were suffering from Frank's expenditures.

He had gone out for a drink and Freda knew she had to do something to get rid of him.

She rang her friend Jane to see if she could call in to see her today. It was only noon now; Frank had gone out as soon as he knew the pubs were open. Jane welcomed her and they sat chatting for quite some time, both were widows and had got together after meeting while standing in line at the local bank.

The knock on the door came at last; the police were very sympathetic as they gave her the bad news. A group of people had been waiting for the traffic lights to change, her son among them, when he had tripped and fallen in front of a lorry. It appeared he had been drinking and must have been unsteady on his feet.

They took her home in the police car. Everyone was very kind to her; after all, she wasn't responsible for her son's drinking habits, was she? After the funeral life settled down into a cosy pattern again.

Freda sat watching the rain pour down outside, she was warm and dry and happy to be alone. Her thoughts wandered to the day of Frank's death. She had been watching as he came out of the 'Black Dog' pub, ready to go on to 'The Fox and Crown', she knew his routine when he went out. It was boring staying in one place, he had said as he told her which pubs he liked to visit.

He had been about to cross the busy road along with a group of shoppers, it was always busy at that crossing. Then she had waited for the right moment and stumbled against the man next to her, reaching through to push Frank into the path of the lorry.

No one had suspected the poor frail old lady with the walking stick; she had been as horrified as everyone else at the crossing. But then she'd made herself scarce, going into the ladies toilets and changing into her own clothes behind the locked door, transferring the 'old lady' clothes into a shopping bag and leaving the stick behind in the washroom.

She was on time at Jane's, and had left a note on the door at home for Frank, telling him where she was and saying she would be home for tea, that's how the police knew where to find her. They hadn't asked how long she'd been there, why should they? It had been a tragic accident.

Just like Sam's, she thought as she watched the rain, only in that instance she had dressed as a man and gone to the cinema afterwards.

I wonder if Frank sees the joke now, she laughed as the rain began to ease and the rainbow appeared. After all, Sam and I were on the stage before he ruined our act with his drinking, and now Frank has followed in his father's footsteps, well and truly.

The End

Laura's Love

A chocoholic gets much more than she ever bargained for when she begins dating a young man who understands her addiction.

As she worked steadily, one thought kept popping into Laura's mind. *Chocolate, chocolate, chocolate.* If only she had some here with her, but it had all gone, eaten at the mid-morning break. After eight years abroad she just could not get enough of her own country's chocolate, how she had missed it! Some of the varieties she had tried in other places were quite nice, but none matched up to her favourite brand. Now she had been back home for six months and the desire for chocolate was still strong.

Across the small office her friend Carol looked up and smiled. "Soon be lunch time and you can stock up again. I've never known anyone who loved chocolate as much as you; lucky for you it doesn't affect your weight!"

The solicitor's office where they worked was a small but pleasant firm to work for, and Laura knew she was lucky to have found this position so soon after returning to England. It was all because her father was friendly with Mr. Allen the senior partner, who'd mentioned that a new assistant was required in his office.

Laura smiled at Carol, "Yes, and Eric is meeting me, it's a lovely day for lunch in the park, thank goodness he can come. I hope he brings some chocolate."

Soon it was lunch time and Laura hurried to the nearby park to meet Eric, she had met him at Carol's birthday party three months ago and they had seen each other regularly since then.

He was waiting for her at the park entrance and they strolled to a vacant bench. Eric grinned as he handed her a bar of chocolate. "It's not for now, Laura, it's for later," he teased.

They ate their lunch and sat talking afterwards, Laura asked. "Shall I see you tonight?"

He looked embarrassed. "No, I'm afraid not, I have to work late but I will meet you here again tomorrow."

After leaving Eric she walked back to the office deep in thought, the bar of chocolate in her hand. Why was Eric always working late these last two weeks? He made excuses not to come to her home and never asked her to go to his, was he going to break things off with her? She began to eat the chocolate as she went into her office engrossed in her thoughts.

"Are you eating chocolate again, Laura? Come on, put it away it's time for work," Carol laughed.

It was hard to concentrate and the large bar of chocolate got smaller as the afternoon wore on. At home that evening her mother said. "I've made a new chocolate dessert for you, Laura, as you can't seem to get enough chocolate these days!" She thanked her mother and after the meal helped to wash the dishes, so busy with her thoughts she missed what her mother had said the first time.

"Are you listening, Laura? I asked why this young man you are seeing doesn't come to meet us, we would make him welcome. Is he afraid of meeting us, or have you not asked him?"

Yes, she had asked him, but he was always busy or so he had said. It wasn't as if she was asking him to marry her, and why had he not asked her to his home? she wondered. But she said none of this to her mother, only promised to ask him to come for a visit, and then excused herself to go to her room.

As she lay in bed later that night—a book in one hand and a bar of chocolate in the other—Laura decided she would ask Eric the next day to come over for a visit. If he made excuses then she would cool down their relationship, after all she was not seeing anyone else because of Eric and she wanted to know what to do.

The next day at work, the morning went by very slowly, only the chocolate in her drawer—which she kept breaking pieces from—helped, they didn't have a lot of work waiting to be finished so they were not rushed.

Meeting Eric in the park for lunch she felt her heart thudding as they sat down, but Eric spoke first.

"I've brought you a new chocolate bar, Laura, do you want to try it?" He handed over the bar wrapped in red, white and blue paper.

She took it from him and with a 'thank you' put it in her bag, then taking a deep breath she said. "Eric, would you like to come to my house tonight?"

His face turned red. "Sorry, Laura, I'm working late. Can we meet on Saturday evening outside the Premier Cinema? There is a good film on that I'm sure you will enjoy. It's a romantic comedy."

Laura stood up. "We meet outside all the time, I have never met any of your family or friends, nor have you met mine. Do you want to stop seeing me, Eric? Am I the one pursuing you? If so we can say goodbye now."

Laura turned to walk away and Eric did not follow. Sadly she went back to her office.

Carol was still there, having decided against going out for lunch. When she saw Laura's expression she went over to her. "Oh, Laura, have you and Eric quarrelled?"

Laura told Carol of her doubts and fears and Carol listened. "But, Laura, you met him at my party! He came with my cousin so you know some of the people he mingles with, don't try to rush things, just let it take its course. In a few months you will be sure one way or another of his feelings, and you can't meet in the park in winter. Here, I brought this for you." She handed Laura a chocolate bar.

It was hard to concentrate all afternoon, but the chocolate Carol had given her helped to lift her mood a little. When they left work that evening Eric was waiting outside for her, and so with a wink and a wave Carol hurried away.

"Don't be upset, Laura, it's hectic for me at work right now, but I like you a lot and I want to go on seeing you."

They walked into the park and sat quietly talking for quite some time, yet Laura felt she knew no more about Eric than before. But the one thing she did know, was that he meant a lot to her. Fearing that she may have lost him after her angry tirade earlier in the day, had made her realise how very much she cared for him. She would take Carol's advice and give it time.

At home that evening she took out the bar of chocolate Eric had given her, it was different to any she had seen before, unwrapping it she broke off a piece. It was really delicious, all her favourite tastes in one bar, wafer, fudge, peanuts, and flaky chocolate, all smothered in thick creamy chocolate on the outside. She gave her parents a piece and they agreed how good it was. Her mother then asked about Eric and looked disappointed on hearing there were no plans for him to visit them.

Saturday came at last, after shopping in town with her mother—during which she searched the shops for the chocolate bar Eric had given her, but no one seemed to know what she was talking about—Laura finally got ready to meet Eric.

As she was putting on her make-up, her mother called her. "Phone for you." It was Eric, saying he was sorry he couldn't make it.

Keeping calm she said, "Fine, see you sometime!" and put the phone down. Nor would she answer when he rang back.

The next morning was bright and sunny, she could see the

sun shining through her bedroom curtains which were not quite closed, and she also saw the chocolate wrappers from the night before on her bedside table.

Going over to the window to open the curtains she realised there was a commotion outside. Funny, Sunday was usually very quiet. Pulling back the curtains she could not believe her eyes. A small crowd was gathered gazing into her garden and the reason was plain to see.

A life size model of herself made from chocolate with a banner behind it saying "Eric loves Laura" was standing there. Quickly she pulled on jeans and a jumper and rushed downstairs, her parents hurried outside with her. She approached the chocolate model in wonder and walked around it. The crowd was growing and people were asking questions but she could not answer them.

Then Eric came down the street carrying the biggest chocolate bar she had ever seen. As he drew closer she saw on the wrapping the words "I love you, Laura. Marry me, please?" A cheer went up from the crowd as he approached, and half laughing, half crying she pulled him into the house.

By this time a policeman was seen coming towards the house, someone further up the road had reported a disturbance, hearing only the noise and not seeing the happy cause of it.

Eric then explained that his father and other family members owned the firm which made the chocolate she liked so much. Yes, he did have to work long hours, but for the last two weeks he had been secretly working on the model of Laura. It had to be when everyone else had finished work for the day, and there had been a few glitches. But with the help of his friends at his father's factory at last it was finished. The final problems had been sorted out last night but had prevented him from meeting Laura.

The chocolate model was still standing outside, as were a growing crowd of people. A knock sounded at the door and the policeman stood there, they explained to him about the chocolate model.

He nodded. "Well, yes, I have seen it, but as it is going to be warm today and it may melt, *and* it is drawing a crowd, I suggest we bring it in." He was grinning as he spoke.

By this time people had appeared with cameras and Laura was photographed standing beside her chocolate double. With the policeman's help it was then carried inside the house and placed where it was cool. Laura was feeling peckish after all the excitement and looked around for a bar of chocolate, after all, she could not eat her double! Her parents were giving the policeman a cup of coffee and talking to him in the next room.

Eric handed her a bar of the delicious chocolate she had tried before but had not found in the shops. "Here you are, Laura, this is our new bar, it's not yet in the stores. Do you like it?"

She took the bar and put it on the table, this was one time

Eric came before chocolate! She went into his arms, holding him close and told him how much she loved him and that she would be happy to marry him.

When everyone had finally gone—and she had eaten her chocolate bar—they decided they would take her giant bar to the local children's hospital, but keep the label with Eric's words to her written on it. The chocolate 'Laura' stood sedately in the corner looking too good to ever be eaten.

Her parents had discreetly gone for a walk after providing coffee for the policeman and a local reporter who had showed up on the scene.

"We are going to market the new bar very soon, Laura; did you like the red, white and blue wrapper by the way?" She nodded, and he laughed. "It's my choice and I have just the name for it, dedicated to you my chocolate loving sweetheart! We will call it 'Laura's Love', people will shorten it down to 'Laura' as they always do with twin-named bars, but you and I will know, won't we?" He dropped a playful kiss on her lips.

Laura's parents returned, smiling at the laughter they heard coming from the room where Laura and Eric sat near the chocolate maiden.

The End

Smoke Screen

*When it comes to saving her grandson, Annie is not the easy mark
her blackmailer expects.*

The night was cold, heavy clouds scurried across the sky and rain was forecast, yet the clouds passed by the little village. Sitting alone in her cottage the elderly woman wondered and waited. Time was important, especially when you were getting older, but there was nothing she could do with time but let it pass as she listened for the footsteps and a knock on the door.

Was it only yesterday that the letter had come? Yet it seemed so long ago. She had just finished breakfast when the post had arrived, nothing much of interest among it except the envelope of a deep blue in colour. Opening it she could not believe what she was seeing, she had tried to read the postmark but it was smudged.

"Tomorrow I will come for ten thousand pounds, if you want to see your grandson again do not tell anyone, just be there with the money."

She read it and read it again, the words sounding ludicrous. It's a joke! He's at college and he'll be coming home at the weekend. If it's one of his friends thinking it's funny they are wrong! she thought. Going to the telephone she dialled the college and after some passing along through a chain of people she finally got Roland's friend on the line.

"I thought you were ill, Roland left a note here saying he had gone to see you and not to worry." Thanking him she made excuses and put the phone down. Where was Roland? Was it a joke? If not, what was it all about?

Since Roland's parents had been killed in a car crash when he was a baby, Annie had brought him up by herself. She was the only grandparent he had. She had always thought he was very much like his mother, the daughter she had lost, and he had never been any trouble to her at all.

But now? What now? After sitting and thinking for a while she decided not to take any chances and prepared to go into the nearby town. The bank released five thousand pounds for her after a little delay, as did the building society when she told them a sad little story of some problems with unexpected bills.

When Annie arrived home she put all the money in a bag and then stashed it away in a cupboard. No more messages arrived by phone or letter but she could not settle all day, waiting for she wasn't sure what, then finally going to bed and having a restless night.

There had been a short note in the post this morning. *"I will collect today."* Nothing more at all, so here she was, still waiting and listening. But today she had not been idle, she had kept herself very busy. Now, sitting near the fire she was ready, the bag nearby in the cupboard.

There was a sound outside, was it footsteps or just the wind rustling in the trees? But then a knock sounded at the door and with her heart thumping she rose to answer it. Slowly she opened the door, a man stood there, he was tall with a hat pulled well down over his forehead, and he wore a long coat and gloves, a moustache and a beard obscured his features. He pushed past her into the room and stood near the fire; she closed the door then moved toward him.

"Where is my grandson? What have you done with him?" her voice trembled.

"Where is the money? Did you get it all?" he spoke in a deep gravelly voice.

"I'll not tell you until I see Roland first; you haven't hurt him, have you?" Annie tried not to show how frightened she was.

"Stupid old woman! I could kill you now then look for the money! Your grandson talks too much about you and what you've got. I have him, he's safe, but I told you to get the money, now where is it?"

Slowly she walked to the cupboard and took out the bag, he grabbed it from her and took out the money. After flicking through it he stuffed it in his pockets. "Never thought it would be this easy," he sniggered, "Your precious Roland is outside in the garden shed."

She rushed past him to go outside and pulled the door closed after her. Running to the garden shed she flung open the door calling her grandson's name. Hearing a faint sound she pulled away an assortment of empty burlap sacks, plant pots and a garden hose.

There he was, trussed up tightly, lying on his side with his mouth covered with a wide piece of tape, she pulled it off and eased him up to a sitting position, getting the garden shears she cut the ropes that bound him and he was free.

"Where is the man who did this?" He wanted to know as soon as he could speak.

"Don't worry," she said as she helped him to his feet. "He is quite safe." They looked toward the house. Every door and every window was covered by a grille, no one could get in or out of there, it was burglar proof. The police soon arrived and had the house surrounded, the man was led out, and yet another surprise was in store for Roland when the man admitted that he was Roland's father. He had not been killed in the car with his mother when it crashed; the other body was some unfortunate stranger to whom they had given a lift. His father had been able to crawl away from the wreckage and had seized the opportunity to start a new life under an assumed name.

Annie sadly told her grandson that his father had always had an eye for the ladies, and had regretted marrying his mother; indeed he'd been having an affair with someone else at the time of the crash. The disguise of the beard and moustache hiding the face of the clean shaven man she had known had fooled her until he had spoken; she'd recognised that horrible gravelly voice immediately.

Things hadn't worked out in his new life and he had come back to try and get money from his mother-in-law in the only way he knew she would part with it. He had struck up a conversation with his son, not revealing who he was, and wheedled his way into the boy's confidence, waiting his chance to offer a lift one night and then kidnap him.

When Roland and Annie were seated in the cottage again and everyone had gone, it all seemed like a very bad dream.

"What about these shutters, Gran? You didn't tell me you had them."

"Well, the salesman offered me a chance to test these new burglar-proof shutters and door locks; they can only be opened with my code both from inside and out. If I allow prospective clients to come around and view them in place occasionally, I can have them for a third of the price if I decide to keep them. I didn't say anything to you as I wasn't sure if I would be keeping them. But I guess we both know the answer to that now, don't we? After all, you can't be too careful, can you?"

As the rain finally arrived, the cold grey night didn't seem so bad after all.

The End

In Between

A near death experience inspires an unmotivated young woman to change her lacklustre ways.

Marie walked with her head down, not really interested in seeing anyone or anything. Was this all there was to life, endless days at the office and endless nights in her small flat?

Ever since her mother had died when Marie was eleven, her life had felt empty, even though she still had her father, a quiet man who had adored her mother. But when his wife died at only thirty-six he had been unable to cope with missing her and looking after his young daughter alone, so he had sent Marie to live with her Aunt Grace, her mother's only sister. Although her aunt was kind and tried to understand her niece, Marie was glad when after passing her exams and leaving school she was able to move out and have a place of her own.

But it was not what she had imagined. No mad social whirl materialized, and it had become a boring round of work and going home to watch television, with a weekend visit to her aunt and an occasional visit from her father.

She would soon be back at her flat now, with nothing to do in the evening ahead but again watch television. As she approached the door of her flat a young woman came towards her. Marie groaned inwardly, not another missionary from a religious group or a sales woman; those were the only visitors she ever got.

The young woman touched Marie's arm, "Excuse me, may I speak to you for a moment?"

"Not just now, thank you," said Marie hurrying on. But the young woman followed her.

"Please, let me speak to you, it is rather important," the woman pleaded.

Well, what do I have to lose, thought Marie, it will help to pass a little time and I have nothing better to do.

"Come along then," she said, and went into her flat with the young woman following. "What group are you representing, or what are you selling?" Marie asked.

"My name is Anthus, and I am here to see *you*, Marie, to give you an insight into the future."

"Well, I don't know how you found out my name but I have no money, so it's no use trying to sell me anything," said Marie.

"No, I am not trying to sell you anything. It has been seen how unhappy you are, and we in the Second Land would like to help you, as we have helped many others before you. Don't be afraid, Marie, sit down and let me explain. What do you think happens when you die? Do you think you go anywhere, and if so, where?"

"Well, I guess I thought you went to either heaven or hell, it's what we were taught in school, but I haven't really thought about it lately," said Marie.

"I am going to take you to the Second Land, it is where people go when they die before going on from there," said Anthus.

"Do you mean that you are a ghost?"

"No, just a being in suspension," said the young woman. "Feel my hand, I am as real as you."

Marie reached forward to touch the hand offered to her, it felt quite ordinary like her own.

"Alright then, I am willing to try anything once, show me this Second Land and what difference it can make to me," she said sceptically.

Anthus took Marie's arm and led her to the middle of the room. "Close your eyes and hold both my hands." Marie obeyed and felt a cold chill creep over her, she clung to the hands holding hers.

Suddenly there were no hands in hers, she opened her eyes in alarm, Anthus had gone and so had her flat. She was standing in an open space, looking around quickly Marie saw that there were no buildings, only people drifting by.

Drifting is right, she thought, they were not walking but sort of floating. Approaching a nearby couple, Marie spoke. "Excuse me, could you tell me where I am?"

The man answered. "Yes, you are on Heedless Plain."

The woman joined in. "Come with me, dear, and we will

show you where to go."

Marie followed the couple, not knowing what else she could do. They went on until they came to a path, and the couple went along it, followed by Marie. Suddenly in front of them was a huge cloud, the couple drifted into it, after hesitating for a moment Marie followed. The cloud billowed about them and before she realised what was happening her feet had left the ground. Whirling around she tried to find a way out of the cloud but it was all-enveloping, there were more people in the cloud and they did not seem worried at all but just stood quietly.

"What is this cloud?" she asked a man nearby.

"It is the Cloud of Nothing," he replied.

Feeling really puzzled Marie realised the cloud was no longer moving. Stepping out of the cloud Marie discovered a river in front of her, grey in colour with wispy trees growing on the banks. Standing on one side of the river was an old man, going forward to join him Marie asked. "What river is this, sir?"

He lifted his head and smiled gently. "Why, my child, this is Nowhere River." And so saying he moved away.

Marie saw a bridge a short distance away going over the river and headed towards it. Two girls got there before her and smiled as she drew near.

"Are you going over Fruitless Footbridge? Then do join us," one of them said to Marie.

Going over the bridge Marie glanced through the rails into the water below, even the water seemed cloudy, she thought. Looking up again she saw in front of her a strange collection of buildings, the girls drifted over to them and Marie followed. The largest building was oval shaped with shutters at every window, all of which were closed.

"What is this building called?" asked Marie.

"It is the Aimless Hotel," said one of the girls nearest to her. Marie wandered through the doors and saw people seated at the numerous round tables; a staircase was on the right and a desk to the left with a man sitting behind it. At last, thought Marie, I can get some sensible answers.

Approaching the desk Marie asked. "Can you tell me where I am and how I get home from here?"

"Certainly, my dear, this is the Second Land and you are in Listless Town. If you wish to return, take the footpath left of the hotel until you come to a gate, go through the gate but be careful, in the field there are goats who like to chase and butt people. If you get across the field there will be someone there to direct you."

Going out of the hotel Marie looked around. How strange, I have not seen the sky since I came here, and I still can't see it now. Even the people look grey, what is it all about? And where is Anthus? She said she had come to help me, but has left me all alone. The other buildings gave no indication of potential help as they were not the conventional buildings Marie was used to seeing, and gave the shimmering impression they would all disappear at any moment.

Turning to the footpath she had been directed to follow, Marie began walking again, realizing she had seen no animals or heard any bird song since coming to this strange place. Striding along the path she saw no one else going in her direction. She touched the branch of a tree in passing and was horrified when it crumbled and vanished before her eyes. Bending down she took a blade of grass and saw it do the same as the branch of the tree. Why is everything here so unstable? I don't like it, at least my job and my flat are solid and dependable, she thought.

There in front of her was the gate at last, she went forward and took off the catch, and slipping inside the field she fastened the gate behind her.

As Marie began to cross the field she suddenly heard the sound of something approaching. Turning quickly she saw two goats rushing towards her, heads bent down and intent upon head butting her. They were upon her before she could get away. She was bumped and butted from both sides; Marie was getting panic stricken when there was a sudden whistle from across the field, and as if by magic the goats moved away. Marie tried to gather her senses, feeling bruised and battered she straightened up and looked across the field. There was no sign of the goats or of whoever had whistled.

I'll go back, she thought, at least I can stay in the hotel and wait for Anthus where she is likely to find me and take me home again.

Turning back Marie heard a deep sigh and as if from nowhere an old lady leaning on a stick stood before her. "Backwards or forwards, my dear, which is it to be then?"

"Which way are you going?" Marie asked.

"Why, my dear, my way is set and this field holds me. I am Mrs. Maybe and I stay here. If you want to return to the hotel, then it is that way," she said pointing, "But if you want to get out of this field then you must follow the path."

Looking to where she was pointing, Marie saw a path leading across the field. She was sure it had not been there before. The old lady was now going in the opposite direction to where the path led and Marie wondered which way she should go. She decided to head back to the hotel, but as she started back she realised the old woman had gone. The field was large and open, there was nowhere for her to have gone. Marie shivered and quickly changed course, deciding she had had enough and would somehow get back home.

As she came out of the field onto a lane a cyclist came towards her. Marie breathed a sigh of relief; at least this was more normal. The cyclist stopped and she saw it was a young man dressed all in grey. *Don't they dress in any other colour?* she wondered.

The young man spoke, "Can I help you? My name is Sometime and I am going to the next town."

"Please, how do I get back to normality?" asked Marie.

"But this is normality for those who reside here. Come with me to Half Valley and perhaps someone there can help you."

Marie felt she had no choice, so resigning herself she set off after the young man, who was now pushing his bicycle.

On the way they passed people wandering along as if they had all the time in the world, no one was hurrying, some were stopping then turning around and going back to where they had come from. Marie was afraid to touch anyone in case they did the same as the branch from the tree and the blade of grass. She felt angry, how could Anthus have been so solid to touch, yet have vanished and left her? In front of her suddenly appeared more buildings, all very fragile looking and appearing to be made from sticks and rushes. Marie approached warily, the cyclist had gone while she had been looking at the strange buildings, it made her very uneasy the way people appeared and then disappeared with no warning.

Standing outside one of the buildings was an official looking man. Marie went up to him. "Is this Halfway Valley? And how do I get back to my own home from here?" she asked.

"Don't worry about getting home, come and let me show

you around our town. I am the leader here."

Before she could answer the man had moved away, so not knowing what else she could do, Marie followed. Walking down what appeared to be a main street the man began talking to her.

"There ahead is Sunshine Road leading to Evening Place, and over on your left is Doubtful Field, behind you are the buildings called Perhaps Block. Down this road you will find it gets wider and brighter, but there is plenty of time to stop and go into any of the buildings you would like to visit. Marie gazed about her, there were vast contrasts from one side of the road to the other, and why such strange names? She decided she would ask her guide.

"Tell me, why are there so many different buildings, and why the strange names? Why did a branch of a tree and a blade of grass crumble in my hand? Yet I have walked into a solid building and have had two real goats butting me, there must be a reason for these things?"

Her guide stopped. "Come into this place we call Deciding Apartments, you can sit down while we talk. I can assure you the chair will not vanish nor will the building."

So they went into the building he pointed to, and there Marie saw a variety of people, some were dressed in grey, some wore pale colours, and some were quite brightly dressed compared to what Marie had seen so far. They sat down in the large room they entered and the man began to talk.

"First of all we need different buildings for all the different people and the forms they take; secondly the names are right for the places and buildings here. You were very careful when you came here and treated everything and everyone with care. But on your way to the field of goats you were thinking only of getting away, and did not think before snapping the tree, you were in such a state that what else could the grass do but follow the branch? The goats you felt were real, but tell me, does it hurt where they bumped you? Have you any bruises, and did you see them afterwards?"

Marie quickly felt her side, no, there was no pain, so almost certainly no bruising. Were the goats then not real?

"Now you are in a building sitting down and it feels real," said her guide. "Trust your feelings, listen and watch with me for a while."

Marie looked across the room, a grey lady was reaching forward to pick up a piece of paper, every time she seemed to have it in her grasp her hand became empty again, over and over again she tried, then with a sigh she drifted across to the door.

Nearby two men were standing together, one was in a pale blue suit and the other was again in grey, as so many of the group were. The man in blue was saying something, but the grey one kept shaking his head. The two men drifted over to the door but only the grey one went out. The man in blue shook his head and made a move to where a lady dressed in pink was sitting.

The lady in pink was holding a flower and smiled at the man in the blue suit, she held out the flower but when he tried to take it from her it fell from his hand after a moment.

"See," said Marie's guide, "If you don't believe in yourself, how can you go on? The lady in grey you saw has been drifting about here for a long time. The man in the blue suit has moved on a little, he tries to make others see now, but he still has a long way to go. Watch the lady in pink."

The lady in pink got up and walked over to where a man and a woman were standing, the man had on a suit that was almost navy in colour and the lady had on a pretty white dress. All three stood talking together then headed for the door, as they went outside Marie could have sworn the pink dress became a dusky plum colour. The sound of their laughter drifted back into the room.

"Come, Marie, let's follow them," said her guide and went to the door, she followed quickly, curious as to where the people were going. Outside the three people were strolling down the street and chatting together, as Marie and her guide drew near they turned off to the left.

Following along, Marie became aware of how light it was becoming, on went the three people they were following. At the end of the street they went into an open space which was light and airy, people were milling about there all dressed in colourful clothing. Suddenly it became bright and shafts of light danced over them, everyone joined hands, the lights stopped moving and a rainbow appeared to settle over them all.

Marie rubbed her eyes, it was a truly wonderful sight, and oh how at peace she felt with everyone and everything. Then as she put her hands down from her face she could not believe it, there was no one there, only her guide remained. She looked around, although the open space was still light and airy, it was now completely empty. Her guide began to walk away, she followed not able to understand what she had just seen.

Back in the main area once again, her guide turned off to the right and led the way into a small building which had a sign outside. Exist House it said. Inside yet again were more people, grey people, pale people, all mixing together, wandering among the tables and chairs set out on the ground floor.

A small chubby man was trying to pull a chair out from under a table, but no matter how hard he tried the chair never moved, his grey suit was creased, he looked worried and finally moved away from the chair. A tall lady in pale green was sitting at a table near the door, she played with a scarf that was draped around her neck, it floated through her fingers.

A small group was gathered in a corner having an animated

talk, they kept shaking their heads at each other, Marie glanced at her guide but he only smiled at her as people kept moving about, never keeping still for very long. Suddenly the group in the corner moved toward the door, as they went outside Marie's guide spoke. "Come on, Marie, let's follow them."

Not knowing what to say, she followed him as he went after the people who had just left. Again they went down the street until they came to the end where an open space waited for them. But this was a grey plain with wisps of cloud hanging in the air, and a certain drabness hung over everything.

People were drifting about here, grey suits, grey dresses. Some dark grey, some a little brighter, all were whispering to each other but no conversation could be heard, only the hushed voices that came over as a sigh to Marie and her companion. There were shrubs growing here and again the wispy trees, no solid oak or tall poplar trees, everything looked as if it would be blown away by a light breeze at any moment. Her guide pointed to the left and Marie looked to see what it was he had seen.

A tall man was walking toward the whispering people, as he drew near they backed away and became silent. Standing in front of them he held out his hands, on the palm of each hand he had pieces of what seemed to be string, lifting his hands he let the strings dangle from his fingers. Slowly a woman walked forward and took hold of one of the pieces, another woman followed and did the same, gradually more and more people came to hold onto

52

the offered strings. Still a few people held back, they huddled together, and all at once drifted backwards down the street until they could not be seen. Marie watched all this, not moving from where she and her guide stood.

The man who held the strings began to move away, as he did so the pieces of string became longer, and the people holding on to them followed him across the space to where the grey clouds drifted along. Soon he and all the people following him were no longer visible. Marie made to move forward but her guide said, "No, don't follow, you won't find them, they have moved on." And so saying he turned and headed back down the street to where they had come from. What could she do but follow him? There are so many questions I need answers to, thought Marie, when we stop then I will ask.

Back on the main street again her guide pointed to yet another building. "The last one for you to visit, it will answer some of the questions you are dying to ask." Together they went inside the building. "This is Middle Towers, and we shall again observe a few things here." The guide went over to where pictures hung on the walls and Marie followed him.

This is like an art gallery, she thought after looking around, pictures filled the walls from top to bottom, there were a few seats and little else. Marie realised that they were not paintings as one sees in galleries, but were all pictures of people. She looked closely at the one nearest to her and was shocked to realise it was her mother. The picture showed a very happy lady with a serenity that was immediately obvious. Marie could not believe her eyes, but there was no mistake. She had a photograph of her mother at home, and even if her memory of the last time she had seen her at eleven years old was a little dim, the photograph was a constant reminder. She turned to her guide, but he had moved away and was looking at a picture further down the room.

Marie could stand it no longer and went to where her guide stood in front of a picture, glancing at it she saw it was of the guide himself.

"Please tell me what this is all about! I can't stand it any longer. What does it all mean? And why is there a picture of you here, and one of my mother further down the room? Can I see my mother? What is going to happen to me? Can I get back home?"

"Marie, one thing at a time," her guide answered. "No, you cannot see your mother, she has gone to the place where all the brightly clad people you saw have gone to. Her picture is here for you to see so that you know she has passed on to greater things, and by the happy expression she wore in the picture you can see she was glad to go. Not that our grey people have a picture in here anyway, they cannot decide so drift on from here and go to Exist House."

"My time here is nearly over so my picture is here for a while, soon I shall also go on to greater things, taking care of you is my last task. We all have tasks to perform here, starting with the small ones, and if we persevere then we go on from there. Do you remember the man trying to pull the chair out from the table? He gave up because he had no faith in himself, and I am afraid he must perform very small tasks and succeed before being given greater ones."

Marie was listening intently to what her guide had said, but he had not told her how she could get back to her own flat in her own town, or what was going to happen to her. Instinctively she knew that she needed to understand this experience before she could leave.

She spoke to him, "I think I understand a little about the people here, please tell me if I am right. Well, first of all many of the people who come here are unsure, they feel lost at being in a strange place, but some of them get used to it and realise they can move on from here to whatever stage is next. How you put the idea to them I'm not sure, but they know. Some of the people here have always relied on other people, so they keep drifting, waiting for someone else to lead them and don't really try to move on. After a time they go to where the open space was, and the man with the strings comes for them, even then some do not make it. What happens to them and where they go I cannot imagine. Some people make no obvious effort, I saw their clothes change colour so I guess they begin in grey clothes, and as they progress they become pale shades going on to brighter colours."

Her guide smiled. "You have the general idea, Marie. Now think of what you were doing with your life before you came here, were you decisive? Did you follow your heart? Achieve your dreams? Or did you wait for life to come to you, for everything to fall into your lap? Were you just drifting aimlessly through your life? I know you lost your mother and that your father could not cope, and by the way, I'm afraid your father will be a grey person for a long time when he arrives."

"To explain a little more to you, yes, people are always surprised and confused when they arrive here, they try to adjust but as you have seen, some people just cannot. They go from this gallery to where their feelings lead them, some to the grey area where some of the people improve. They go on from there and get better after making their first effort, even then some slip back."

"Those who go from here with any colour at all try to help those with none, as you perhaps have seen. People drift here for a long time if they do not trust themselves, and after a while they are drawn to a place where they are met, given a line to grasp and taken to where they will always be doubtful, not trusting their own feelings, but will have someone who will help and guide them."

"Those who gain their colours back are drawn to the place where the rainbow descends, then lifted to the Glorious Land, there happiness awaits them. Those who could not even grasp the line given by the person on the grey plain are doomed to become the wisps of cloud you saw hovering about. Now, Marie, my time is

56

over and I must go on from here, do not forget to trust your feelings, don't drift. Farewell for now."

So saying the guide headed for the door and went outside, Marie hurried after him but as she stepped out of the door, Anthus suddenly appeared in front of her. Marie was so startled she forgot to go after the guide.

"Where have you been, Anthus? How could you leave me here? I want to go back to my own flat in my own land," said Marie.

"Tell me, what you have learned? Are you going to be as decisive with everything as you seem to be now? And how do you know you can get back at all?" replied Anthus. This was a complete surprise, was she then a grey person without realizing it? Glancing down Marie was horrified to see she resembled the grey people she had been watching.

"Am I… am I a… *grey*…?" Marie could not finish, but looked towards Anthus who was holding her hands out to Marie.

"Come, Marie, you will see, follow me and I will show you." So Anthus went out of the gallery and down the street with Marie following her.

They passed many buildings and soon came to the end of the street, but Anthus did not go around the corner, she stopped and entered a very shabby looking place. Again it looked as if it would fall down at any moment. Marie followed Anthus inside what seemed to be no more than a hut and was amazed by the bright light that met her, and for a moment she could not see Anthus. Blinking hard she could just make out the shape of Anthus kneeling down and gazing into what appeared to be a pool in the floor. Joining her, Marie knelt down beside her and looked into the pool, this was where all the light came from, it was as if a thousand mirrors shimmered from the pool, it was a beautiful sight.

Looking into the middle of the pool Marie was amazed to see it suddenly become clear in the centre, and a picture appeared where seconds before it had been shimmering. There was the road where she lived, a car and a bus were parked and a lot of people were standing about in groups. She heard a voice drift to her. "Poor girl, she never looked. I saw her walking with her head down and she stepped right in front of the bus, the car had to swerve to avoid hitting the bus. Why did she walk about with her head down? It wasn't the bus driver's fault he hit her."

The picture changed and Marie saw a hospital, a single bed in a stark white room and a doctor leaning over someone in the bed. That someone was her.

"Well, I'm afraid there is nothing more I can do," the doctor said. Marie lifted her head and gazed at Anthus.

"Does it mean I am dead?" she asked.

Anthus rose from beside the pool. "Listen, Marie, some people who come here go straight from here to the Glorious Land,

58

but even those people sometimes do not enter there, but only get to the Gates of Welcome, they are then returned to their past lives having had a brief glimpse of what is to come. Then there are people like you who come to us for a visit but are not ready for anything more, they are in suspension. Remember, Marie, your life is yours to live, trust your feelings, lift your head and meet life or it will not be there, it will be too late."

"Do you mean I am not dead, but in what did you call it… 'suspension'?" asked Marie.

"Yes. Now is your chance, you will remember very little of what you have seen but the lesson will remain with you. Take my hands and come with me," said Anthus.

Marie reached out, but found when she tried to grasp the hands offered to her that there was nothing to hold. She tried again with the same result, then she thought of her own flat, how lucky she had been, but how lethargic by not going out to meet people, instead just sitting and waiting for everything to come to her. Well, I will be different now, she vowed, and felt Anthus gripping her hands.

Marie closed her eyes as the hands in hers tightened their grip; there was no sensation of falling, flying, or moving at all. But somehow Marie knew she was no longer in the hut. Opening her eyes she saw the doctor standing by the bed that she was lying on, her hands were being held not by Anthus but by her Aunt Grace.

"Oh, Marie! I thought we had lost you, your neighbour in the next flat told the police where I lived and they came for me, thank goodness you will be alright! She will be alright, won't she, doctor?" Her aunt turned her worried gaze from Marie to the doctor.

The doctor smiled, "Well, it's amazing, but I am pleased to say Marie stands a very good chance of a full recovery, she has a couple of cracked ribs and a concussion," he said as he turned to look at Marie, "But my word, you are a lucky young lady! Not many people could have survived being hit by a bus. The only thing that saved you was the bus was slowing down near one of its stops, and that you were thrown onto the pavement and did not fall under the wheels. But now it's time for rest, and when you wake I'm sure you will be feeling better—apart from the aching ribs and a headache—of course." The doctor said wryly, and with a laugh he ushered Marie's aunt out of the room, and after a quick check on her vital signs he left Marie to rest.

She just could not believe it, here she was in a hospital bed! Where had she been? Was it a dream? How could it all be explained? Funny, her ribs hurt where the goats had butted her! A hundred unanswered questions buzzed around in her head, which hurt and throbbed. Slowly Marie drifted off to sleep, her last thoughts being of how she would join the local badminton club where she could meet people, and would go to an evening class, pursue her hobbies, learn to dance and also perhaps do a little

60

charity work. There was so much she could do with her life—so very much.

The End

A Lady of Merit

A sweet and gentle love story involving Lady, a lovable dog and the humans who adore her.

Striding down the country lane, Richard was feeling that life was very good, the sun was shining and the air was clear, here in the countryside everything smelled fresh and clean. So different from his flat in a busy city where traffic roared past in a never ending stream and you heard the sounds of the people in the surrounding flats.

This break from the city was just what he needed, although he had to admit that when he had been offered a two week break here, he had at first refused, wondering what on earth he would do with himself for two whole weeks.

He had been here for three days now, and the peace of the countryside had overwhelmed him. How grateful he was to Adam his friend at the office who had offered the use of the cottage to him. It belonged to Adam's parents and was their weekend and holiday retreat, but after Richard's recent illness Adam had offered it to him for a 'breather' before returning to work. Now Richard was settled in and feeling better already for the peace, the relaxation, and the fresh air he was getting. The only thing I am missing is a dog at my heels, thought Richard as he strolled along.

The thought had barely crossed his mind when a golden Labrador shot out of the hedge in front of him and came running up to him, it stopped, wagging its tail and looked expectantly at Richard. There was a sound of running feet and then a shout of

"Lady, Lady, where are you?" and out of the hedge bounded a young woman.

She was slim with dark curly hair, brown sparkling eyes, and, Richard guessed, about five feet three inches tall. She came hurrying toward Richard and the dog, her flowered cotton dress billowing in the gentle breeze.

"Come here, Lady! I am sorry, she gets so excited when we come out, has she been bothering you?" she asked.

"No, not at all, she only just got here, but what a lovely dog she is," said Richard.

"Well, usually she is quite good when she is out with me but I guess she knew someone else was here today, we don't usually meet anyone around here," volunteered the girl.

"I'm here for two weeks at Laurel Cottage; it's not my place but belongs to a friend of mine. By the way, my name is Richard Taylor."

"Hello, my name is Susan Hudson, I live with my parents across the fields at the Angel Inn, it is fairly quiet here except for the locals and the occasional visitor, but it's a good place to live."

"Yes, I can believe that. I haven't been to your inn yet as this is only my third day here, but I feel so much better already, I shall come by tonight," smiled Richard.

"Well I hope you enjoy your stay here, now Lady and I

must be going," said Susan.

So bidding each other goodbye they went their separate ways. Richard went back to the cottage and thoughtfully made himself some coffee. Susan was not a bad looking girl. He had been content during his first two days to just stroll about the lanes and woods, and then in the evenings sit reading and relaxing, but tonight he would go to the inn.

The rest of the day passed in a peaceful way, lazing about in the garden, getting a meal, and exploring another path around the back of the cottage which led to a little pond.

So came evening and Richard prepared to go to the inn, he was going to ride down the country lanes on the bicycle which Adam had told him was kept in the shed outside. After checking the lights and brakes Richard set off. Going along at a steady pace he soon reached the Angel Inn. Putting his cycle round the back he went inside to the bar, there were a few people inside, all looking as if they were local residents, having an air of ease about them.

Richard ordered a drink from the landlord who was a cheerful red-cheeked man with a shiny bald head and quite inclined to talk to this stranger, saying that he hoped Richard's stay would continue to improve his health. He had another customer to serve and Richard went to sit down at a corner table.

Susan suddenly appeared behind the bar and smiled as she saw Richard. As she came forward to greet him Lady squeezed past her and came over to Richard, sniffing around his legs as he patted her, and then settling down at his feet.

"Well, would you believe it? I know she is friendly but she has only just met you," said Susan.

"I'm glad she likes me, she is a lovely dog. Can you stay and have a drink with me, or do you have to get back? I will understand if you can't sit with customers," said Richard.

"But I can, as you see we are not really busy and I only help out if we get a lot of visitors coming in, my job is outside of the village, I am a secretary but I'm at home for three weeks as I've had a bout of flu. My doctor said I needed rest, so here I am," Susan smiled.

They sat chatting away with Lady lying between them on the floor. Richard briefly told Susan about his job, of his interests in art and reading, walking, and sometimes photography.

Susan returned the information with her own. She was twenty-two and a secretary in the nearby town, her parents were wonderful, that's why she commuted each day to work, they allowed her all the freedom she wanted. Her interests were swimming, walking with Lady, painting (though not very well), she admitted, and tennis.

So they chatted along about their work and interests until Susan's father called her to say that her mother wanted her. Richard fetched himself another drink and returned to the table where lady was still lying on the floor.

Soon Susan returned and Richard fetched her a drink too, they continued chatting for some time and then it was time for Richard to cycle back to the cottage. He asked if he could see Susan again, and they agreed to meet the following morning to walk Lady. Richard rode away in a euphoric state which had nothing to do with the two drinks he had consumed.

The next morning he was up bright and early, and after eating his breakfast he decided he must tidy the cottage in case Susan came over, not that Richard was untidy, but dusting and vacuuming were not things he thought of very often. Today however, he busied himself with the tasks and the cottage looked all the better for it.

Then it was time to go and meet Susan. As he walked down the lane where they had first met yesterday, Richard pondered on how strange life was. This time yesterday he had been quite content to be alone, yet today he was eagerly looking forward to meeting Susan. They arrived at almost the same time and smiled at each other a little self-consciously, Lady ran around their legs in high spirits as they set off to walk together.

After a while they relaxed a little more and began to chat easily to each other again, as they strolled along Lady followed behind, occasionally dashing into the undergrowth to search for whatever it was she imagined was there. They came to a little pond and stopped to rest, sitting side by side. Richard felt so content and amazed at his luck in meeting someone so special.

They eventually wandered back to the cottage where Richard made coffee for them both, not forgetting to give Lady a bowl of water, he thanked his stars he had tidied the cottage before inviting Susan back there.

Then he realised what Susan was saying, she had a boyfriend of sorts, at least they had grown up together and everyone thought of them as a couple. Richard felt his heart sink, but managed to smile and keep the conversation going, no, he told her, he had no girlfriend, female friends yes, but no special girl of his own.

Susan was getting ready to go and Richard walked with her down the lane, saying he would see her that night and foregoing the kiss he wanted to give her. The rest of the day seemed long and not very interesting; he moped about and could not settle to anything until, at last, it was time to go to the inn.

When he walked in after leaving his bicycle around the back, Richard saw Susan was already there, but not alone, a young man was sitting where the night before he had sat. Going forward to the bar he heard Susan call his name.

"Richard, I'd like you to meet Mark, his father is the local doctor here and Mark is studying to become a doctor as well. He is home for a few days before going back to college."

Susan smiled as she told Richard all this, and Richard politely went forward to meet the smiling young man.

Mark was stocky and dark haired with brown eyes like Susan's, he was a contrast to Richard who was tall, fair, and had blue eyes. But the big smile and hand held out to him melted Richard's resentment as he went forward and shook hands.

"Pleased to meet you, Mark, I'm just a city dweller down here for a short stay."

"Hello there, Richard. I hear Lady has taken a liking to you, my word you are honoured, she is a very choosy lady!" Mark laughed.

They all sat down and began to talk, try as he might Richard could not dislike Mark and found him most pleasant. Susan joined in the conversation and Lady lay under the table. After a while Richard said he should be going, not that he had to but who wanted to play gooseberry all night, certainly not him.

So he rose and bidding goodnight to them all, he went out to get on his bicycle. Riding back to the cottage he pondered on the cruelty of fate. To find a girl like Susan, be so happy, only to realise she belonged to another.

After a restless night he got up early and made some coffee for himself, while sitting drinking it in the living room he was surprised by a knock at the door, going to open it he found Mark there.

70

"Hello, Richard, sorry to bother you so early but it seems there is a child missing from the village. No one realised last night as she was sent to bed early for being naughty, but it seems she slipped out in the night and she is only seven years old."

Richard quickly let Mark in and after telling him to help himself to coffee he went to get dressed. When he returned Mark explained that the whole village was searching for Sarah the missing girl and the two went out to join the search.

First of all they searched all the outside area around the cottage, not forgetting the shed where the bicycle was stored. Then they moved further away and began looking in the fields, but there was no sign of the missing child. As they walked carefully looking everywhere around them, Richard and Mark talked. Mark told Richard how fond he was of Susan, how they had grown up together and how they had each gone on to their respective careers. Richard explained how he had come to be in the countryside to recuperate and how he loved it here.

"You would not say that if you lived here full time, Richard, there's no entertainment around here, only the village inn," said Mark.

"After living in the city, it's heaven for me," replied Richard.

They had walked some distance now and they came upon other people from the village also searching for the lost girl. Susan and Lady appeared, hurrying up to them Susan told them how they had searched everywhere except the woods, and they were all going there now.

Off they all went with Lady leading, they began to search the woods, splitting up to do so, but it was Lady's bark that drew everyone's attention, she had reached the pond before them and as they all rushed forward they could see that she had found something. The young girl Sarah was cowering under a bush, and only came out when Susan came to help her. She had been cross at having to go to bed early, so had decided to run away, but having got into the woods she had become lost in the dark. Everyone was so relieved that she was alright that no one scolded her at all, and they all set off back to the village with Lady having special cuddles for her find, and Sarah being carried by one of the men.

Richard made his way back to the cottage, unable to help himself from wondering if it would be fair to try to entice Susan away from Mark, but knowing he would never try to do such a thing. What a start to the day, he thought, but it was not over yet.

After having some breakfast Richard decided to go for a walk and finish up at the inn for lunch, so he set out. As he went he reflected on how much he liked Susan and decided he would cut short his holiday and go back to his flat at the weekend and not stay for his second week. Walking into the inn he went to chat with Susan's father at the bar. He was his usual amiable self and quite willing to talk with Richard.

72

There was no sign of Susan or Mark anywhere, so after getting a sandwich at the bar and having another drink, Richard headed home again. When he arrived he found Susan and Lady waiting for him.

When they were inside the cottage there was an awkward silence for a moment, then Richard told Susan he was going home at the weekend.

"But that's only two more days, I thought you had another week here!" Susan exclaimed.

"Well, I am better now so I may as well go back, not that I don't like it here, I do, but I have no reason to stay," Richard smiled, "But thank you for everything, Susan, making me feel welcome and walking with me."

Susan smiled back, "Well, Richard, please take care of yourself, won't you." They shook hands and Susan was gone.

On Saturday Richard was all packed and ready to go when he heard a dog barking outside. He hurried to have a look; it was Lady in the nearby woods barking frantically. Richard raced in the direction of the noise. Lady was standing near the pond still barking and nearby lay Susan. Richard ran forward, there was no movement from the girl at all.

Carefully he turned her over, but there was no response. Checking for broken bones and finding none, he then lifted her and carried her back to the cottage with Lady dancing at his heels.

Gently he laid her down on his bed and went to fetch a damp cloth which he placed on her forehead, he saw as he did so the lump on her left temple, so it seemed Susan had struck her head on something. Lady lay near the bed looking with anxious eyes at Susan.

Richard sat beside Susan holding her hand, after a little while her eyes opened and she tried to focus, then as Richard spoke she seemed to realise where she was.

"Susan, thank goodness you are alright! I was so worried, but I didn't dare leave you alone to go for a doctor, but now I can see you are a little better I am going to fetch him."

Susan gave a weak smile. "I fell and banged my head. Oh, it hurts! How long have I been here?"

"Not long, but no more talking now, just rest. I am leaving Lady to look after you, I will be as quick as I can." So saying Richard hurried outside, got the bicycle out of the shed and pedalled furiously toward the village.

He went first to the inn and banged on the locked door. Susan's father appeared and Richard rapidly explained what had happened, also wanting to know where he could find the doctor. In no time at all Richard, the doctor, and Mr. Hudson were all on their way to the cottage, the bicycle being left at the Angel Inn.

Susan was still lying on the bed with Lady at the bedside, but Susan appeared to be asleep.

74

Dr. Dale went forward to examine her while Richard and Mr. Hudson went to wait in the next room. They just sat watching the door, neither of them speaking until the doctor came out.

"Nothing serious, no great harm done. What she needs is plenty of rest, don't move her for a while yet," he said.

Mr. Hudson went in to see Susan; Richard hung back and asked the doctor if he would like a hot drink. Making coffee for them all gave Richard something to do and he was surprised to find his hands shaking as he made the drinks. Mr. Hudson came out and said Susan was resting comfortably, so feeling relieved, they all sat down to drink their coffee. Lady would not leave the bedside however, not even for a bowl of water and a treat so Richard quietly took them in to her.

There was a knock at the door and when Richard answered he found Mark there with Mrs. Hudson, he let them in and Mrs. Hudson hurried through to see her daughter.

Richard gave Mark a cup of coffee, and the doctor said he must be going but would look in again later. Mr. Hudson again thanked Richard and said he would have to get back for opening time at the inn, so now that his wife was here he would leave with the doctor. Richard saw them out and came back to talk to Mark.

He began by saying what a good dog Lady was and how devoted she was to Susan, and Mark agreed. Richard then asked how long Mark and Susan had been going out together, he was startled when Mark laughed.

"Going out together? Why, Susan is like a sister to me! She has always been around, we have grown up together. I've just come to make sure she is alright, I care about her very much but only as a brother would."

Richard felt his heart lift, did Susan feel the same way or was she in love with Mark? After all she had said she had a boyfriend 'of sorts', could it mean she cared for Mark more than he did for her? How Richard wished he could go in to see Susan now, but Mark was still speaking.

"I'm having a good time with the rest of the students, when we are not studying we go out and have fun, no getting serious with anyone for me until after I qualify as a doctor."

Mrs. Hudson came out of the bedroom and again Richard offered coffee.

"Mark, you can go in now but not for long, she is very tired after that awful fall," said Mrs. Hudson. Mark went to the bedroom door and disappeared inside to see Susan, how Richard wished it was him!

Sipping her coffee Mrs. Hudson turned to speak to Richard. "What on earth was Susan doing out there? Thank goodness she had Lady with her and that you heard Lady barking. Thank you so much for taking care of her."

Richard found he was completely at ease with Susan's
76

mother and had soon, he realised, told Mrs. Hudson his life story.

"Well, fancy you and Susan both being here because of a bout of flu, that's what I call providence." Richard saw that Mrs. Hudson was smiling as she spoke.

Mark came out of the bedroom. "She wants to see you, Richard," he said.

Richard felt his heart thumping as he entered the bedroom, he went over to Susan carefully stepping over Lady on the way. Quickly he took Susan's hand.

"How are you? Is your head still hurting? I am so glad you are alright."

"Richard, please listen, Mark and I have been talking. I thought he was in love with me and did not want not hurt him by saying I only loved him as a sister would. I have been trying to think how I could get you to stay, that's what I was doing this morning, walking and thinking when I tripped, fell, and bumped my head. But Mark has just told me he loves me as a brother would and no more, we are *both* so relieved and happy. Mark can go back to his studies and I, well, it won't hurt Mark whatever I do."

Richard reached forward and took Susan's other hand also. "Do I have a chance then, Susan? I know I have only just met you but I would like to get to know you better."

Susan held onto Richard's hands. "I liked you from the moment we met, and Lady never gets it wrong where people are concerned, she would have ignored you if she had not felt you were a good kind person."

At the mention of her name, Lady came to the bed and jumped up beside Susan, wagging her tail. As he held Susan's hand and stroked Lady, Richard felt that this was the start of something wonderful.

The End

And So, To Bed

A practical joking brother finds that the joke is on him.

Judy and June sat with their mother listening to the radio; it was a program on music past and present which they all found interesting. Mrs. Grove liked hearing all the 'old songs' as her daughters called them, while they at fourteen and sixteen preferred something more modern, and quite a discussion had taken place on which music was the best.

George, the eldest at nineteen was at work with his father, they both did the nightshift at the local colliery, and the youngest son David was in bed.

The program ended and June gave a yawn. "Well, I'm off to bed now, are you coming, Judy?"

"I guess so, at least it's Saturday tomorrow, so no school for us. Are you coming to bed too, Mum?"

"Yes, Judy," her mother replied. "Now just remember you have to use a candle in your room tonight, your dad will repair the light fixture tomorrow, those frayed wires aren't safe. It will be alright when Dad has sorted it out, so it's only for one night."

Both girls kissed their mother goodnight and went upstairs, June carrying a lighted candle balanced on a saucer. When they got to the top of the stairs they turned to go along the landing to their bedroom. Suddenly Judy grabbed June's arm, coming towards them was a white figure with arms outstretched. June gave a yell and fled through the nearest door into her mother's bedroom closely followed by Judy. They scrambled under the bed with the candle flickering and almost going out.

"Why didn't you put the light on, June?" hissed Judy. "It's only our room that has the faulty light fixture!"

"Because I'm as scared as you are, and I didn't think of it. But hiding under Mum's bed won't help though, will it? What was it?" June demanded.

"A ghost? Let's yell for Mum and David and see if they can help us," Judy whispered.

They shouted together, the candle casting flickering shadows on the wall as they did so. Suddenly the sound of laughter stopped them and the door opened, the light came on, it was David and their mother who laughed even more at the sight of the two girls scrambling out from under the bed.

June was furious. "It's George again, isn't it?" She went to her older brother's bedroom door at the end of the landing, there hung one of her mother's cotton nightdresses, the long sleeves outstretched with a broom handle holding them out. The breeze from the open window swayed the 'ghost' towards her. "That blasted brother of ours! If he's not putting spiders in our beds or jam on the door handles, it's this sort of thing!"

"Sorry, June," her mother said, "but he made me promise not to say anything. Don't worry, I'm sure you'll get your own back on him!"

David removed the 'ghost' and eventually they all calmed down enough to go to bed and sleep. The next day, Saturday, there was no work or school but George and their dad would need to sleep after working all night, so after June and Judy had told their big brother what they thought of him—and he'd had a good laugh—they went out shopping with their mother while the men went to bed and David went to play football.

At tea-time June tried to catch out her brother by putting ice cold tea in his cup, and replacing the sugar in the sugar bowl with salt, but he was ready so any tricks did not work. Their father said they must all stop. "No more of it, behave like grown-ups all of you!" he admonished.

George went to get changed for his night out with his friends, but before he left the house he couldn't resist just one more joke. His friend at work had loaned him a skeleton made of plastic, but it was very real looking. He crept up to his sisters' room and carefully hung it on the window. When they came in and went to pull the curtains they would have a surprise, especially as Dad hadn't fixed the light fitting in their room yet, so it would be candle light again for them tonight.

George had a disappointing evening, his best friend didn't meet him and after talking with a group of his workmates at the pub for a while he decided to go home. The girls were still at the cinema and David was staying with a friend overnight, so only his parents were at home. They played cards for a time, then the girls

82

came home and after a lot of banter they decided to go to bed. George listened with a grin on his face, and sure enough the expected yells came from upstairs.

"One day, George, your jokes will rebound on you," said his father as he headed upstairs, "Let's see what you've done this time."

All three climbed the stairs; George hurried on ahead laughing and went into his sisters' room. Sure enough, they were cowering under the bed covers. He quickly lifted the skeleton down, rattled it and moaned, and then his father came into the room.

"It's only another of George's jokes, girls, come on out of there."

June and Judy were furious with George and vowed they would get even with him. But their mother quietened them. "Come on now, the neighbours will think this is a madhouse, let's all go to bed."

"I'll turn off the lights when I've had a hot drink, you all go to bed… and mind out for the *ghosties*, girls!" said George. Both girls made a dash for him, but he disappeared down the stairs in a flash.

Parents and daughters settled in their bedrooms hoping to sleep, but no one was ready after all the excitement. They heard George locking up and switching the lights off.

George made his way to his room and pushed open the door, he started, then laughed, his sisters had said they would get even but this 'white ghost' they had fixed up for him was so obvious!

He walked towards it. "Well now, what have they made you from?" he said stretching out his hand, but his hand moved through the ghostly shape as though there was nothing there. A shiver ran down his spine. Gradually the white mist enfolded him and he began to float and gasp for breath. He thought he heard an echo of his father's words, "One day your jokes will rebound on you." But he couldn't think anymore, only float, just float.

The End

Mr. Bates

A widower enjoys his solitude and a very singular hobby, until burglars interrupt his quiet world and get the surprise of their lives.

Mr. Bates was a quiet man and all his neighbours knew that, no one ever saw him doing or saying anything out of place. Since his wife had died five years ago he had been seen less than ever. A retired office worker and not a very important one at that, Mrs. Bates had been known to complain about her husband not getting on as well as he should at work, 'always letting others get promoted over him' was how she'd described her husband.

Now he was alone, no children to visit and seeming to go out only for a walk in the local park or to get his weekly groceries. People in the row of houses where he lived sometimes commented to each other and wondered how on earth did he manage to pass the time? But any offers of help or friendship had been gently but firmly turned down by Mr. Bates.

Today the sun was shining, it was a bright May morning and Mr. Bates stepped outside to go for a stroll in the park. He hurried along, head down, a small figure with a trilby hat hiding his bald head. The park was quiet, the children were at school and only a lady walking her dog and a tall man with a walking stick passed him.

He sat on a bench to rest before going home again and considered the little problem which had been worrying him. The front bedroom was now full, his own bedroom was too small to put any in there, the loft he could no longer climb into, his sitting room was too cluttered with furniture and no matter how he tried, there didn't seem to be any way he could add to his collection because of the shortage of space. His latest delivery might have to be his final one. If he had collected something simple like postcards or stamps it would have been easy, but no, he hadn't, so there was the problem.

After a while he got up from his seat feeling chilled—it was still early May and could be cool despite the sunny day—and slowly walked home.

He had just put his key in the lock when a voice made him jump. "Hello, Mr. Bates, are you alright? Would you like to come round for a cup of tea?" It was Mrs. Lomax from next door, didn't the woman ever give up? Even when his wife had died she had not been inside his home or he hers, but the curiosity she so obviously felt about him showed very clearly. Her husband was still working and with her two children living in the next town, time hung heavily for Mrs. Lomax.

Mr. Bates turned and smiled. "Thank you, but I am alright and I do have things to do. Good day to you, Mrs. Lomax." He quickly turned the key and went into his home.

Had she seen the crate arrive yesterday? Every time he had a delivery she was there trying to get into his home, or coax him into hers to find out anything she could. He had a light meal of beans on toast with a cup of tea, and then got to work. By teatime it was finished and he looked at his handiwork with pleasure.

It was a comfortable home but getting quite crowded now, maybe a bigger home would solve the problem.

The next day was a shopping day, so he went along the road to the bus stop, going into town to the supermarket was a nuisance but his wife had never wanted them to have a car, and now that she was gone it was too late for him to start driving. By the time he had returned home with the shopping he felt very tired and was glad not to have Mrs. Lomax call out to him again.

After putting his shopping away and eating his meal he began on his hobby again, surely he had more here than he remembered? He tried counting them but it was no use, he just lost count every time. They all looked very good though, peak condition he felt, and all the attention he had given them had been worthwhile. He went from room to room looking them over and feeling quite pleased with himself.

An early night was called for after his shopping trip, so he was in bed by ten o'clock. He was aroused by a sudden noise, was it a burglar? He felt his heart begin to thump.

Getting out of bed he crept downstairs, yes, the noise... a rustling sound, was coming from the kitchen. He held the heavy torch high ready to strike whoever it was, but when the kitchen door began to open he found himself going to hide in the sitting room instead. There was the creak of a loose stair board—he had avoided it coming down knowing which step it was—as the intruder went upstairs. He heard his own bedroom door opening and stayed where he was, and then there was a movement at the top of the stairs as the burglar went into the second bedroom.

His heart racing he hurried upstairs, grabbed the handle of the bedroom door, turned it and locked it with the spare keys he had picked up on his way through the sitting room. Keeping locks on all the internal doors had been a good idea after all, he thought as he hurried back downstairs to call the police.

There was a crash from upstairs as the burglar stumbled around in the dark; he had not bothered to replace the bulb in the second bedroom as he didn't go in there after dark anyway.

The police were prompt in response to his call to say he had caught a burglar. The noise from upstairs was quite loud. Two policemen went into the bedroom and brought out a man who looked as if he had just woken from a bad dream.

"Your spare stock you keep in there, sir, it really upset him!" said one of them as they helped the burglar downstairs. Mr. Bates just smiled as he saw them on their way.

When they had gone, saying that they would be back the next day for a statement, he went into the spare bedroom with his torch and put a bulb into the light fitting. Then he began to tidy his models. There were arms and legs everywhere, but soon all was as it should be, or nearly.

He had used the clothes for his ladies that his late wife had collected for her women's charity group. She had died suddenly before handing them over for the Autumn Fair. Good quality they were too, from the big houses on the hill. He had nearly given them to the Salvation Army along with his wife's clothes. Then he'd had his idea of having the perfect female companionship.

His wife had never given him a moment's peace at home, now he was surrounded by model ladies who never nagged, but just stayed where he put them with no trouble at all. It had been a good idea buying ex-mannequins from a supplier when they were past their best in the shops. Always company for him, he could change them around when he wanted, but he would have liked to have seen the burglar's face when he was trapped in a room full of them.

Well, tomorrow he would sort out his ladies, and chuckling to himself he went back to bed.

The End

Strange Happenings

A young reporter is sent to investigate strange happenings in a small quiet village, and discovers a whole lot more than he bargains for.

The day was bright and the sun was shining as Stuart drove along the country lane. He felt a little tired, it was warm in the car, so keeping his right hand on the wheel he reached over and wound down the window on the passenger side. Now he had a through breeze to help him keep cool and alert.

He thought about what he was doing here, the call to his editor had started it all. A lady had telephoned about strange happenings in the village of Marston, which was ten miles from the town of Allwich where Stuart lived and worked.

He was a bachelor of thirty. A fairly good looking man with blue eyes and sandy hair, quite content with his single state. Stuart had always wanted to be a reporter, he remembered starting work as a general assistant, making tea and coffee, doing all the menial tasks and working his way up the ladder. Now he was a respected senior reporter, living in a flat with his cat Jason.

He had been sent to investigate this story by his editor who wanted something to spice up his newspaper. Stuart had instructions to try and bring back a good reliable story, so he had booked into the local inn for three days. There was not a lot of information so far, Mrs. Sims had been hesitant on the telephone, saying she would rather talk face to face about what she had seen.

Stuart saw Marston coming up in front of him, he drove down the main street and turned right past a row of cottages until

92

he saw a big white house at the end of the road.

He pulled up in front of it, and getting out of the car he went to the front door and knocked. It seemed ages before it was answered, slowly the door opened and a middle aged lady stood there.

"Yes? What do you want?" she asked suspiciously.

"Are you Mrs. Sims? My name is Stuart Reynolds of the Chronicle newspaper, you rang us about a story, so I'm here to talk to you," Stuart said.

"Oh, do come in," she said standing back for him to enter.

They went into the sitting room, it was a cosy room, very pleasantly furnished where Mrs. Sims told Stuart to sit down.

"Would you like to tell me about the strange things that have been happening?" asked Stuart getting his notebook and pen ready.

"I'm sure you will think I am mad when I tell you, but other people have seen the same things as me and are too frightened to speak out," said Mrs. Sims. "It all began about three months ago when I was in my garden at the back of the house doing some weeding. Well, it's very private and at the bottom of the garden are woodlands, no one else was about, it was very peaceful but I suddenly felt as if someone else was there."

"When I looked up there was no one there, but near the

trees was a strange light, just like the beam from a torch reflected on the trees. Suddenly it grew brighter and bigger, a form began to appear in the centre of it and a man stepped forward out of the light, he looked at me and then vanished. I rubbed my eyes, looked toward the trees but there was nothing unusual to see at all. Well, I decided I had been in the sun too long and went indoors."

"The next incident was a week later, I had gone for a walk with my dog, we stopped for a rest down Natchers Lane when Sam's hair suddenly stood up on his back—he is very good at letting you know if anyone is about—so I looked around to see who it was. Again there was this light which grew then the man stepping out of it only to disappear. I began to think I was going mad! Sam was whimpering and I felt afraid too, so we hurried home."

"My friend, Mrs. Eleanor Slater came for coffee the next day and I told her what I had seen, knowing she would not tell anyone. To my surprise she told me that a similar thing had happened to her, we exchanged ideas on what we thought it was but could not really decide on how to explain it."

"Over the next few weeks we found that more people had seen the same thing, we all got together and I said I would contact your paper, but everyone disagreed, they thought we would be branded as mad so the idea was abandoned."

"But after my experience of two days ago, I made my mind

94

up that something must be done, so I contacted you," she took a deep breath and continued. "I was in the village when the man who had come from the pool of light passed me, he did not disappear, and then I noticed more and more strangers in our village, I felt something was going to happen and was frightened."

"Well, nothing happened on that day, but the next day as I went into my garden the man was there. I spoke to him but he didn't answer, he just stared and pointed at me. All at once I felt a warmth around me, I knew I was in a circle of light as he had been, I felt myself getting lightheaded and euphoric, it was easy to slip into a happy carefree state but I thought of my home and I fought against it, there was a loud bang and I found myself lying in the garden. I got up, ran inside and locked the door, but nothing else happened. I feel frightened in case it happens again. I wonder if anyone else has experienced it, and if so did they fight it? And if not what happened to them? Well, what do you think of my story, Mr. Reynolds? What should I do?" finished Mrs. Sims.

Stuart sat for a moment trying to make up his mind, was this a crank who wanted publicity? Or was it a woman who really believed what she was saying? He decided to play along for the time being and see what else he could find out, so he said, "Could I see your garden where it happened?"

They went out into the garden. Everything looked perfectly normal, the wood was at the bottom of the garden. Stuart walked down the garden path and climbing the fence went to look at the trees. He walked around the ones nearest to Mrs. Sims garden, searching for signs of anything unusual. But it was on one of the trees that he spotted something, it was a deep green tinge around the trunk of one tree. He moved closer to examine it, bending forward he touched it with one finger, it felt greasy but as he looked at the green mark on his finger it suddenly disappeared. He stared at his finger then at the tree, yes, the green looking mark on the trunk of the tree was still there. Suddenly he felt the hair on the back of his neck stand up, looking around quickly he saw only Mrs. Sims standing in her garden watching him.

When he looked back at the tree the mark was gone, he could not believe it! He went to look at the other trees nearby to see if he could see anything on them, all the while the feeling of unease persisted but there was no sign of anyone else nearby.

Finally he went back to join Mrs. Sims, she looked at him, "What did you find then? I saw you touch a tree and look at your finger, was there something there?"

"I'm not sure, I would like more time to make up my mind," Stuart answered.

He took his leave of Mrs. Sims promising to come back again, and then made his way into the village.

Strolling down the main street he passed a few people who appeared to him to be furtive and afraid, everyone seemed to be hurrying along as if they could not wait to get home.

He stopped a man coming along the pavement towards him; rapidly he explained who he was and why he was in the village. The man looked afraid but spoke to Stuart. "There are some strange things going on here it's true, but no one can put their finger on it, we are frightened to try to do anything because we don't know what we are up against."

"Have you ever spoken to these people who are appearing in your village?" asked Stuart.

"No, it's the way they look at you, as if telling you not to approach them, no one I know has spoken to them. Now, if you will excuse me, I must be going." And the man hurried away.

As he watched the man go Stuart again felt all the hair on his neck standing up, a cold feeling swept over him, but on looking around he could see nothing to account for it, everything looked perfectly normal.

Deciding he needed to know more, Stuart made up his mind and went to the public phone box, he called his newspaper and spoke to the editor, saying he would be staying to investigate further and promising to check in with more details later. Then Stuart headed for the local inn.

There he spoke to the landlord about a meal, and having disposed of that little matter he then asked him about the strange new people in the village. A wary look crept over the man's face and he said he knew nothing as no strangers had been in for a drink and he himself never really went out and about in the village being too busy running his inn.

Stuart could see he was not going to get anywhere, so he thanked the landlord and went outside. The main street was almost empty, but as he went down the street toward the row of cottages before Mrs. Sims's house he again felt the prickling sensation and uneasy feeling he had experienced before. There was a man coming towards him, very well dressed and striding out as if he knew exactly where he was going. As he drew near, Stuart put out a hand, "Excuse me, sir, may I speak to you?"

The stranger looked at Stuart, there was something in that look, a contempt, a dislike, an aloofness and more, a strange feeling came over Stuart as the stranger looked into his eyes, then moved on. Standing there Stuart felt mesmerized, he did not call after the man or make any move after him, he just felt that he couldn't or shouldn't. Slowly the feeling wore off and he continued on his way, arriving in front of Mrs. Sims's house feeling rather foolish. Mrs. Sims answered his knock at the door and ushered him inside, he related his encounter with the man and she nodded her head.

"Yes, I know what you mean. Who are they and what do they want? Everyone here is frightened of the men, they never speak but always seem to be around, no one knows anything about them."

Stuart nodded his head. "It is a mystery, but one I shall try to solve. I am staying in the village for a few days to see what I can find out."

They sat chatting together for a while, and then Stuart rose to go after asking Mrs. Sims to ring him if anything unusual should happen.

Back at the inn he went to his room and began to write a report on the happenings so far. It made strange reading, nothing concrete but a lot of things that were not normal.

Stretching himself, Stuart finished and put his report away in a drawer, he decided to go down to the bar and get something to eat. The landlord supplied sandwiches which Stuart ate in the lounge of the inn. He again tried to hold his host in conversation about the strange people but without success. There was no information to be gained at all and Stuart felt very frustrated, how could he clear up the mystery if no one would cooperate but Mrs. Sims? She seemed to be his only ally.

As if in answer to his thoughts the telephone rang and the landlord informed him Mrs. Sims wanted to speak to him. She sounded very nervous but excited as she asked him to come to her house, saying she would explain all when he arrived.

Stuart set out at once and quickly arrived at the white house, but there was no answer to his knock at the door, he tried again, but no response. So he went around the house to the garden at the back.

As he drew near the bottom of the garden he again felt the hair on the back of his neck standing up, and the same uneasy feeling flooding over him. There was no sign of Mrs. Sims, but as he looked at the trees beyond the garden he saw a green light, as he drew near the light got brighter and bigger until it looked like a huge translucent balloon, in the middle of which was a dark shape. Stuart stopped a few feet away from it, and fascinated, he stared, waiting to see what would happen. The shape was now as big as he was, it started to move, gliding over the grass until it came to a big tree nearest to Mrs. Sims garden, and there it stopped.

It was now completely still, the light from it glowed brighter and brighter, Stuart covered his eyes, he could not stand it. But when he lifted his hands from his face he was amazed to see the bubble and the light were gone and only an empty space remained, but on the big oak tree the green tinge was there.

Stuart went to touch it, and as before it came off the tree onto his finger, but even as he looked at it, there was nothing there, it had gone. He became aware of a voice calling him, it was Mrs. Sims in her garden, he went towards her wondering if he had dreamed the bubble, the light, and the green tinge on the tree.

"Were you out here, Mrs. Sims? I came to see you but there was no answer when I knocked on the door," said Stuart.

She smiled, "No, I haven't been anywhere, perhaps you

didn't knock on the door hard enough, would you like to come in?" They went into the house, there Mrs. Sims quickly provided coffee and Stuart told her what he had seen.

To his surprise she laughed. "I think you must have had a little nap on my garden bench while waiting and had a dream! By the way, I found out who all the strange men are, they are thinking of building a huge shopping complex here. They are surveying the area to see if it is the right place for it, progress you know, Stuart, we can't stop it!"

Stuart was puzzled, he knew he had knocked hard on the door, yet she had not answered, and here she was in a completely different frame of mind to the last time he had seen her.

Further conversation showed that Mrs. Sims had brushed aside any thoughts of strange activities and was prepared to think it was a lot of fuss over nothing.

Feeling far from happy, Stuart left. Why had she changed her mind? He determined to come back when it was dark and keep a lookout himself, there was something funny going on here, he just knew it.

So he sat in his room at the inn, going over his notes on everything he had seen and heard until it was dark, then he put on his coat and headed back to Mrs. Sims's house.

There was a light on in the downstairs room but Stuart did not knock at the door, instead he crept around the side of the house into the garden at the back. All seemed still and quiet, there was no sign of anything near the trees at the bottom of the garden. He settled down to wait behind a bush, time passed by and he began to feel cold and stiff, suddenly he became aware of a door closing, then he saw Mrs. Sims coming down the path, she passed by where he was hiding and went toward the trees. There she stopped and touched a tree, nothing moved, but then a green tinge appeared on the tree, then a glow of light appeared and a bubble formed and grew, as it expanded Stuart saw something in the centre of it, Mrs. Sims had not moved but stood watching.

The bubble was now like a big balloon, getting bigger and brighter all the time. Stuart determined that he would not close his eyes this time, but found the light so unbearable it was impossible to keep looking. As his hands came up over his face he again felt the prickling sensation and disquiet he had experienced before. Then a feeling of being lifted up in the air, a rushing sound, a feeling of falling, a cold sensation and then nothing.

When he opened his eyes it was to see not the garden but bright lights everywhere, he was lying down on what seemed to be a metal bench, looking around he saw the walls were also metal, and the ceiling and floor too, with only the lights to break up the area he was in.

Nothing moved, no one was there but himself, he tried to get up but however hard he tried his body would not lift from where he was lying. A light appeared in a corner and began to get

102

brighter as he stared at it in horrified fascination. Then the bubble appeared which grew and became brighter still, with something inside it. Slowly it glided over to where Stuart lay; he closed his eyes against the brightness, his arms refused to lift up for him to cover his eyes.

The large bubble stopped beside him, and as he squinted at it the light dimmed, the bubble separated and out stepped a man, the bubble faded before Stuart's eyes and the man stood looking down at him.

When the man spoke it was like listening to an echo, a strange voice, unreal and eerie.

"Why do you hide to watch for us coming? What is it you want? We are peaceful and mean you no harm, it is not good that you write a report in your notebook about us."

Stuart stared at the man, his mouth had not moved yet the words were very clear.

The man passed an arm over Stuart and he found himself able to move as the stranger's arm went from the top of his head and moved over his entire body.

"I am a reporter for a newspaper, it is my job to find out anything that is different and report back, we heard of strange happenings so I was sent to see what was going on here in the village, and why people are so disturbed. Who are you and what do you want?" Stuart said.

"We are here to see how Earth people live. To watch and learn before returning to our own planet, but we chose too small a place this time. If we had gone to where you have many buildings with a lot of people perhaps no one would have noticed us, but here they see everything. We had to bring the woman here and teach her not to talk about what she has seen; now she accepts us." Again his mouth had not moved but Stuart heard the words clearly and he understood why Mrs. Sims had changed her mind, also why these people never spoke to the villagers.

If these people had indeed gone to a city they would not have received the attention they had attracted in the village.

"Will you let me go now?" Stuart asked the stranger.

"We need to first ensure you will not tell everyone about us," his captor replied.

Before Stuart could do anything the man's arm came up again, and try as he might Stuart could not move. Suddenly out of the ceiling came two long metal arms, they fastened themselves to his body, one on his legs, the other on his chest, a bright light shone on his face and a buzzing noise began to get louder.

Stuart felt he would go mad, and gave himself up to the light and noise until he was conscious of nothing else. All became still and he felt as though an implement was probing his brain, it was too much and he slipped into unconsciousness.

When he again opened his eyes he found himself lying in

104

the garden, he struggled to a sitting position and held his head in his hands. Had it all been a dream? He felt very strange and disorientated.

Getting to his feet he slowly made his way back to the inn, where he went to his room and lay upon the bed. He found himself thinking that tomorrow he would go back to Allwich and tell his editor there was nothing worth writing about here in Marston.

The next morning as he prepared to leave, the landlord informed him someone wanted to see him. Stuart went downstairs to find the first man he had spoken to in the street waiting for him.

They sat at a table near the bar and the man who said his name was Jim Gregory told Stuart why he wanted to see him.

His story was also of being plucked up by the alien visitors, but he had fought the lights and had pretended to be unconscious before he was dumped back in the village.

"We have to find this ship of theirs," said Jim, "and then we may be able to do something."

Stuart felt the adrenalin pumping and all his thoughts of leaving vanished. He realised the aliens had underestimated a human being's tenacity and endurance, and felt that, yes, they must do something.

So he asked Jim to call a meeting of the villagers in the hall at the end of the village for that evening. He called the landlord over and asked if he was prepared to help or not. The landlord agreed he would inform his customers of the meeting and warn them to be careful of the aliens, and ask everyone else to pass the word on. Now Stuart felt all fired up, and parting from Jim he went to see Mrs. Sims.

She was in her garden when he arrived and greeted him with a smile. "Hello there, are you going home today, Stuart? Do come in and have a coffee before you go."

How did she know he was thinking of leaving? He just smiled and followed her indoors.

The coffee was soon served and Stuart knew he would have to be careful what he said. So he told her he had given up and was going on to a more interesting story elsewhere. They parted company amicably and Stuart went away more determined than ever to see this thing through to the end.

The day dragged by, he tried to find other people to speak to in the village, but there seemed to be more of the strange men about and he did not achieve anything.

At last evening came and Stuart prepared to go to the village hall, he hurried down the main street, there were none of the strange men about, in fact there was no one about at all, the street was deserted.

The hall was well lit and when he opened the door he was surprised to see how many people were inside. Going to the front of the hall he found Jim Gregory there talking to some other men,

Jim introduced Stuart, then holding his hand in the air called for quiet and declared the meeting open.

Stuart explained who he was and why he was there, and then asked for information from the villagers. There were many varied accounts of the sightings of the light, the bubble which grew and the men who stepped out of the bubbles. The fear of everyone in the hall of the unknown was palpable. Some people had experienced the same as Jim and Stuart and had fought it, they were here to tell their story, but how many of the villagers who were not present had succumbed to the aliens? Mrs. Sims was one at least.

It was then discussed what the intentions of the aliens might be, perhaps they were only observing, but with what in mind? Did they mean to take over the Earth? Or to take people back to their own planet? Perhaps they intended to enslave humans or kill them? The comments flew back and forth among the villagers. Stuart called for order and asked if anyone had reported the happenings to the police or any other official body.

Yes, some of the villagers said, but the messages had never reached beyond the village.

"Well the question now is what to do, and I think the first thing is to track down the space craft, it must be right near the village and you locals may know the most likely places," said Stuart.

Jim agreed to organise search parties the next day, and it was arranged to meet the following night in the hall to see if the space craft had been found.

The villagers drifted away, it was obvious as they left that they felt more hopeful than when they had come in. After talking for a while to Jim and the men who were with him, Stuart said goodnight and went outside.

As he walked down the street he had the same strange feeling he had experienced before when the aliens were near, but glancing around he saw no sign of anyone at all.

Going into the inn Stuart headed for his room, it would be a busy day tomorrow, an early night would not hurt. He went to the drawer where his notes were, intending to check what he had written but there was nothing in the drawer, trying to keep calm he went through all the drawers, but there was no sign of the report he had written.

Well, I know who will have taken it but they can't take it out of my head, he thought angrily.

Did these beings, whoever they were, really think they could control people's minds and mould them anyway they wanted to? Well, they would not find it so easy, Stuart decided as he prepared for bed.

After a quiet night he rose early, once dressed he made his way downstairs, in the kitchen he made tea and toast which he sat

108

down to enjoy.

The landlord came in, "You are up early, are you going back to town today?"

"I haven't decided yet, but I thought I would look around while it is quiet," Stuart replied.

The landlord had not been at the meeting last night and after his initial refusal to talk, Stuart was wary of confiding everything to his host.

"Well you will certainly find it quiet at this hour, it's a fact." So saying the landlord smiled and went out of the kitchen.

Leaving the inn and going down the street it seemed his words were true, not a soul was in sight as Stuart walked along. He headed for Mrs. Sims's house determined to search the woods behind it.

Going into the woods he carefully looked about him, all was quiet, no signs of any movement anywhere. Methodically he made his way into the woods scanning the trees for any signs of the green tinge he had seen before. Deeper and deeper he went, but nothing strange was to be seen, suddenly he heard the sound of twigs snapping, someone was coming, quickly he hid behind a large oak tree. Into sight came four men, but Stuart sighed with relief when he recognised Jim, and stepping out from his hiding place he greeted them.

"Good morning, I see you too are early, Jim."

"Oh, Stuart, I didn't expect to meet you, we are searching the woods and the fields on the other side, do you want to join us?" asked Jim.

They went on together, all the men looking for any sign of anything unusual. Much later they stopped for a rest, having combed the woods and seeing that the fields in front of them appeared to be clear.

They agreed to split up as they were now in the open, and Jim went with Stuart, the other three going off together. Crossing the fields they kept a sharp lookout for anything out of the ordinary, but nothing was seen. They came at last to some rough wasteland, Jim spoke, "No use even trying to get over there, Stuart, there is only an old quarry there beyond this waste ground, even our visitors could not land a space ship there."

But Stuart was not convinced, "Let's go a little further and see if there are any signs of them," he said. They struggled across the waste ground; all five men were now together again and were watching to see if anything strange was in the area.

At last they came to the edge of the old quarry, looking down there was nothing to be seen except the marks where digging had taken place in the past.

Jim and Stuart decided they would scramble down anyway, and their three companions said they would search the area around the top of the quarry. Slipping and sliding they carefully descended and finally came to a stop in the bottom of the quarry.

They set off looking for anything that might suggest someone or something had been there. Further and further they went, suddenly Jim grabbed Stuart by the arm and pulled him behind an outcropping of rock. They both peered around the side; Jim put his finger to his mouth thereby telling Stuart to be quiet.

The sight they saw was amazing, the bubble moving over the ground came to a stop quite near them, before their eyes it grew, but no one stepped out of it, it kept on growing until it was as big as a small house. Suddenly a grey mist covered the inside of the thing in front of them, Jim and Stuart stood mesmerized by the strange happening. The mist cleared and the thing had shining lights of green, red and blue, glowing and then dimming all around it. An opening suddenly appeared in one side of it and gliding out came bubble after bubble; they moved over the ground then floated up the side of the quarry and vanished from sight.

Jim and Stuart stared at each other, neither daring to speak, a sound made them turn their heads, the lights had gone from the thing in front of them, a grey mist again covered the inside and a swishing sound came to the men as they crouched in hiding.

They watched as slowly the thing shrank down in size to become a bubble which then glided away.

Quickly Stuart motioned to Jim and they began to follow the bubble, stealthily they crept along watching and listening all the time. It drifted along until it came to a crevice in the middle of the quarry where it eased itself inside.

The two men were astounded by what they had seen, they silently crept away and went to where they had clambered down into the quarry. Gradually, step by careful step they made it to the top of the quarry, and then looked for their comrades of whom there was no sign.

A whistle from the fields alerted them, they hurried off in the direction of the sound and their comrades emerged from their hiding place.

"We thought you had been caught, we saw all the bubbles and hid ourselves until they were gone, we were coming to look for you when you reappeared," Paul the youngest of the three men said.

"You'll never believe what we found," said Jim, and he told the three men what they had seen in the quarry.

"Well, now that we know where it is we must do something, it's my belief it must be while the space craft is in its enlarged state and we can see what we are dealing with," said Stuart.

They made their way back to the village and Jim agreed to contact everyone and tell them there would be another meeting in the village hall that night as there were new developments, no mention of finding the space craft would be made until everyone

112

was present.

Stuart felt uneasy as he left the other men, would it all go as planned? Would the villagers rally around to do something about the space craft and its inhabitants? Would the beings— whatever they were—be aware of something happening? Surely with such intelligence as they had shown they knew something was going on in the village, what would they do to counteract it? What could they do? No one really knew the full power they possessed, did they?

It was a worried Stuart who rang his editor and told him the story was still developing, Stuart knew if he told the full story there would be armed forces, weapons, military vehicles… and everything required for a national emergency. He felt it would be a mistake, and that many lives would be lost if a full scale outcry was raised. So he told his editor only that he was on to something. And after all, if the villagers had not been able to summon help from the police, his call for help would no doubt be blocked by the strangers too, and now Stuart felt that it was his fight, his and the villagers.

That night he made his way to the village hall still feeling uneasy but determined on a plan of action.

There were quite a few people there, Jim was waiting for him and also Mrs. Sims was there. Stuart looked at her as Jim came to greet him, but she just smiled and waved, which did nothing to help his unease at all.

Having conferred with Jim they both made their way to the front of the hall, apart from evicting Mrs. Sims, which he knew he could not do, there was nothing that could be done about her presence at the meeting.

Everyone went quiet as Stuart raised his hand for silence. He told his audience as concisely as he could what he and Jim had discovered. There were cries of anger and amazement at the way the aliens had hidden their space craft, followed by calls of what should be done about them.

Suddenly Mrs. Sims stood up. "Don't be fools, accept the inevitable, we are not the master race! They will be kind to us and care for us if only we do as we are told. They need to take many things back to their own planet, including some of us, but no harm will come to anyone if you obey."

There was a shocked silence at this outburst, everyone was staring at Mrs. Sims, then through the door came a line of the strangers, all looking so normal in their suits they could have been going to a business meeting. They moved to the front of the hall and faced the people.

Not one of them opened his mouth, yet the words came out clearly. "You cannot succeed, we are here to stay, at least until we have finished what we set out to do, we shall be in control here, you will not ruin our plans."

114

The stranger nearest to Stuart lifted his arm. It was obvious he had been giving the instructions, everyone was staring in a horrified way at him, no one moved or spoke.

"In a few days we will be ready, and then we shall select those who will go with us. We have samples of your other kinds of life here, we do not want the large species you keep in the green areas surrounding the towns, but we have smaller types and will use them as we need to," the words came from the alien.

Suddenly there was a scream from the back of the hall. "You beasts have my cat! I know you have, she never goes far away from me yet she has been missing for three days now!" A woman was standing shouting the words.

The alien pointed his hand at her, she stopped moving her arms in mid-air, her mouth remained open but no sound came out; she appeared to be rooted to the spot. Everyone clustered together in alarm, no one speaking.

The alien spoke again. "Do you not realise that we are far above your intelligence? We can destroy you if we wish, but we are not destructive, we only wish to carry out our mission, which is to see what life exists on other planets and to take samples back with us for experimentation. You are of low intelligence, did you not know we were aware of your search for us? We saw you find the place where we are hidden, but nothing you can do will destroy us. Have we not assumed your shape and voice while we are here?

Nothing is beyond us."

Stuart found his voice. "Why are you all in the guise of men? And who are you taking with you when you return to your planet? Will they be returned here?"

The alien voice came again. "We will not reveal who we are taking or why we are as your men are, no one who goes with us will be returned."

There were fearful whisperings among the villagers now, who would be chosen and why? There was nothing they could do. The alien lifted his arm, the poor woman who had been concerned about her cat suddenly gasped and sank into a chair.

"Remember, defiance is futile, we will leave here soon with those we need, until then do not try to resist us." He walked to the door followed by the rest of his group.

Stuart wondered what the alien would have done if anyone had tried anything. There was a deathly hush, then everyone began talking at once, most agreeing that it seemed there was nothing to do but comply with the aliens. Stuart called for silence, and when they were quiet he began to tell them what it meant if they did comply. Husbands, wives, children would go, never to be seen again, and who knew what awful experiments they had in mind? Did they want that for their loved ones?

There was a murmur of dissent followed by cries of 'Well, what can we do about it?'

116

Looking around Stuart saw that Mrs. Sims had gone, as had a few other villagers he realised. So he began to explain what happened if they remained strong and in control of their minds and did not let the aliens take control. He told them how he himself had initially failed, but how Jim had succeeded, and he felt it was the only way the aliens could be beaten, by everyone concentrating their energies together. His plan was for everyone to meet the following day at the quarry, to put their minds to defeating the aliens and pray that it worked.

After some discussion they all decided they had little chance of a better plan, or any other plan at all, so it was agreed they would all meet at ten in the morning at the village hall before going to the quarry, each one knowing that tomorrow could be their last day if the aliens decided to destroy them for defying their rule.

It was a very troubled set of people who went their separate ways that night, Stuart not the least, he felt responsible for the lives of all these people.

After a very restless night he awoke early and paced his room, going over and over everything, seeing if he could think of anything else that would help to overcome the visitors. He finally gave up the idea and went downstairs to try and eat some breakfast before going to the hall to meet the villagers.

When he arrived at the village hall he was surprised by how

many people were waiting. It was as if everyone had called on their reserves of determination and strength, they all looked ready for the word go.

Stuart explained what he had in mind. They would all go to the quarry and line up at the top of it, and then they would all exert their minds to concentrate on the aliens and not allowing them to take over. If anyone succumbed to the power of the visitors the rest of the villagers would ignore them and carry on. No one would give in without a fight, no doubt the aliens would be aware of the intentions of the villagers, for as the leader had said they were far above human intelligence, but the villagers must try to defeat them anyway.

Everyone looked apprehensive but all agreed with Stuart, so they gathered into groups and set off for the quarry. Mrs. Sims was not among them and Stuart assumed she was now completely in the aliens power after her outburst at the meeting last night.

As they approached the quarry with Stuart and Jim leading, everyone was on guard, yet when it happened they were almost taken by surprise. A line of bubbles suddenly floated up from the quarry. Gathering his wits Stuart called, "Quick, don't let them out of their covers!" He ran forward grabbling Jim by the hand, everyone joined hands and tried to encircle the bubbles, but it didn't work. As if they knew what the villagers were doing, the bubbles rose in the air high above everyone's heads.

"They must land before they can get out of the bubbles, quick everyone to the quarry!" Stuart moved as he spoke running to the edge of the quarry. Everyone followed and the bubbles drifted to the ground behind them.

Breathless and panting the villagers lined the edge of the quarry and stood hand in hand, the bubbles were behind them, the quarry in front, what chance did they have now? Stuart wondered.

"Get ready, we are striking a blow for everyone, not just ourselves, concentrate with all your might! Think of your home, your family, your friends and what this wonderful planet of ours means to you, we are not giving it up so easily are we? Let's put up a fight!"

The bubbles behind them were growing as Stuart spoke, and he knew the men would come out of them soon. Well we are as ready as we can be now, he thought.

There was a whooshing sound and suddenly hovering over the quarry was a giant bubble, it stayed in mid-air as if watching, and the bubbles behind them kept growing. Stuart shouted a last word of encouragement as the men appeared from the bubbles and moved forward.

There was a grim look of determination on everyone's faces as the men came closer, one of them lifted his arm and pointed. A woman further down the line suddenly let go of the hands she was holding, quickly the men who had been on each side of her joined their hands together, pushing the woman to the ground. Another of the men in suits lifted his arm and pointed, this time at Jim, nothing happened and slowly the one who had pointed came to a stop. His companions kept on moving forward, pointing as they did so, another woman cried out and let go of the hands she was holding, but again the circle was repaired by those on each side of her. In all, five people now lay on the ground, but only a few of the men in suits were still advancing, the rest stood as if turned to stone.

"Keep it up!" Stuart yelled as the villagers stood their ground, and slowly but surely every one of the men in suits came to a stop.

The villagers let go of each other's hands, jumping up and down and yelling with joy until a call from Stuart brought them up short.

"It's not over yet, that thing is still watching us, join hands again quickly!" He pointed up to where the giant bubble had begun to glow red and green. Everyone went back to their original positions, watching the space bubble warily.

Then it began to move over the heads of the villagers until it stopped where the men in suits were unmoving. A beam of light came from underneath it, it traced over the heads of the men, and as the light moved back and forth the men vanished to be replaced by the bubbles, which slipped into the beam of light and went quickly up into the giant bubble which was their space craft.

All was quiet for a few moments, then a noise so high pitched it was almost unbearable came from the craft; arms were dropped as people reached up to cover their ears.

"No, No! Think of your homes, your families! Grit your teeth, but join hands again," shouted Stuart. He knew how hard this would be, but if their thoughts were not concentrated the aliens would win.

Quickly everyone joined hands again as the noise rolled around them, some who could not stand it fell to the ground covering their ears, but the breaks in the chain were again quickly filled as they stood determinedly together against the awful sound.

As suddenly as it had started it stopped, and everyone recovered enough to re-join the chain which spread across the top of the quarry.

From the space bubble a voice came. "You who are the leader, we wish to speak with you."

"Well then speak!" shouted Stuart.

"Come to us here and we can speak together, remember that we can kill you all if we wish," the voice replied.

"Don't go, Stuart! They may not let you come back," Jim urged.

"I must go, if I am not back within the hour it's all up to

you, Jim," said Stuart.

A long metal arm came down from the space ship, Stuart walked forward, it picked him up around the waist and lifted him up. Inside the ship it was all metal. Stuart looked around for signs of life.

The disembodied voice spoke again. "You have disturbed our plans, why do you do this? There is so much life on your planet, no one will miss the few that we take. We have seen how they live and what they do; your lives are empty and have no meaning. We are trying to improve lesser beings such as you, and your planet can also be vastly improved. We wish to begin by looking at what you call the brain, there is so much work to be done there, you waste so much time on things of no importance. If we can improve the humans we take we will return for more, there are so many, why does it matter if a few leave with us?"

Stuart realised that emotions were not a part of the makeup of these visitors, no wonder they could not cope when everyone put thoughts of love, devotion, trust and loyalty in their minds.

He tried to explain but realised it had not been understood, so instead he asked what the alien proposed to do as they were not willing for any human to leave Earth, humans were important to one another, he told them, and even one would be missed.

There was silence for a moment and then the voice said, "We need someone, if no one will come willingly then it must be

122

you, or all these people will die."

Stuart wondered how he was going to get out of that, he did not want everyone to die, but nor did he want to be a human guinea pig for the aliens.

So he asked for time, promising he would return that night. The alien did not understand the concept of a promise but agreed to allow him to leave, warning him that if he did not return by darkness the village would be destroyed.

Stuart was lowered down to his friends, and quickly explained what had been said. The space craft moved over the edge of the quarry and vanished.

Everyone made their way back to the village hall. Stuart outlined his plan to Jim and the villagers, and they hastened away to do his bidding.

The day went by very quickly and it was soon time for Stuart to return to the quarry. He set out alone, and as he walked he thought about the few words that had brought him here in the first place. He had said he would help these people and he would do so.

The quarry loomed before him and soon it would be dark, he stood on the edge waiting for the space craft, it appeared very suddenly hovering above his head.

"Well, have you prepared to come with us?" the voice came from above.

"No, he hasn't, and neither have we," shouted the voice of Jim.

People appeared from everywhere, holding hands and all walking to the quarry. They converged on Stuart, his hands were grasped and held as hundreds of people filled the area, they all stood still gazing up at the craft, defiance on every face.

There was a whirring sound, blue and green lights flashed, the space craft moved lower, hand in hand the people lifted their linked arms, they were concentrating on all that was important to them.

Slowly the space craft descended until it was in front of the people, a voice came to them, weaker it seemed now. "We do not understand how you can do this, our power is mighty, we have conquered other worlds but they were not humanoid like you, we have much to learn but though we will leave for now, we shall return."

"I advise you not to return here, we have what you do not— emotions—which can be very powerful, this will always be so! Do not return here, and before you leave return our other life forms," said Stuart.

A sliver of light appeared in the bottom of the craft, and a gap, through which appeared cats, dogs, birds and other small creatures. The people watched, still holding tightly to each other's hands, having been warned by Jim that they must do so, there would be time to find the animals later.

The gap closed and the craft rose and began to hover over them.

"Do not think we are finished here, we shall return when we have learned more, then we shall rule you all. You took our strength, we cannot destroy you, but remember we will return," the voice came to them on the night air, as it finished speaking the space craft swooped away and was quickly out of sight.

There were shouts of joy and relief, Jim and Stuart hugged each other and everyone was chattering all at once.

Jim had done what Stuart had suggested, contacted all the friends and relatives of the villagers, therefore making more minds to join forces against the aliens.

They felt that if the authorities had been brought in the aliens would have just destroyed everyone; at least this was a peaceful end to the problem with no loss of life.

They all made a pact to search the quarry the next day just to make sure of course, then hopefully life would return to normal.

The next day Stuart went to the quarry with Jim and others from the village, there was no sign of anything at all to be found. They agreed all was clear and headed back to the village.

Mrs. Sims was waiting for them; she apologized for what she had said at the meeting, saying it was as if someone else was in her head, which in a way was true Jim said.

So now Stuart must ring his newspaper, but what could he say? And how did he explain not calling the authorities? Would anyone believe emotions were stronger than weapons? Well, he would just have to do his best, and he was a reporter with experience, so he felt sure he could put a story together.

He had learned a lot from this experience, made new friends, and now had a lifetime interest in the village of Marston.

And all because of a call about strange happenings.

The End

Time Goes By

*A young childless couple think they have their future mapped out,
until a young boy warms their hearts.*

Why was it that some days seemed longer than others? Take today for example, she had been busy all day, cleaning, polishing, and getting the house spick and span, yet it was only three o'clock now. Pauline sighed as she looked around the home she and Bob had created from a two up, two down cottage. And what a state it had been in when they had taken it over.

They had worked hard to make it into the comfortable home it was now, the pale blue in the sitting room that merged into a darker blue in the dining room, the gentle magnolia paint and flowered bluebell wallpaper in the upstairs rooms. How carefully they had chosen the furnishings, paint and paper, and all the little extras that spoke of it being theirs.

Bob would not home for two hours yet from the school where he taught, and time often seemed to drag these days since Pauline had lost her job with the estate agent where she used to work due to the cut-backs caused by the recession.

Blasted recession, she thought, if only I could get a job! But she knew there were a lot more like her all looking for work. She was lucky really, at least they had saved when both of them were working and they could manage on the wage Bob had, some poor souls were really struggling.

If only she could do something, but voluntary work wasn't up her street and she didn't really want to get involved with other people. She and Bob liked to keep to themselves, they were everything to each other, they had even decided they didn't want children. Her parents had both been dead a long time, they had left her with Aunt Lucy overnight whilst they went out to celebrate their wedding anniversary, and there had been a car crash that had killed them both instantly. She had been just three years old at the time. Even Aunt Lucy was now gone after a short illness last year, so she had no living relatives—only Bob who she loved dearly.

Bob himself had come back to Britain from Canada where his parents had emigrated soon after their marriage, so he had no one here either. His brother and sister had stayed near their parents in Canada, but he had wanted to come back to England to decide for himself which country he would prefer to be in. He had met Pauline after qualifying as a teacher and decided to settle where he was.

Suddenly her train of thought was broken by a knock at the door, she groaned, "I'm not in the mood for dealing with salesmen today."

Opening the door she was surprised to see a small boy. "Can I have my kite, missus?" he asked. "It's stuck up your tree." She looked down the path to the tree at the bottom of the small neat garden. When they had first moved here five years ago Bob had wanted to chop the tree down to allow more sunlight into the house, but she had said no as it gave her a feeling of being settled and belonging, and of bringing a part of the past with them into the future. He had laughed and willingly left the tree.

She walked down the garden path with the small boy following. "We just moved here last week," he told her, "my name is Peter, I'm seven. How old are you?"

Pauline had to smile. "Well now, ladies don't usually give their ages away but as you told me yours I'll make an exception, I'm twenty-seven."

"That's *really* old," said Peter as they stopped at the tree.

"Yes, it is—so don't go telling anyone!" she said, trying not to laugh.

The kite was tangled in the branches of the tree and would not be shaken down. Having got the ladder from the shed in the corner of the garden, Pauline put it against the tree and climbed, her new neighbour watching from below. After some struggling— with advice being given by Peter—at last the kite was freed. When the ladder was put away they went into the house to try to untangle the string.

"Won't your mother wonder where you are, Peter? You really shouldn't wander off alone you know."

"Mum is asleep and Dad is at work. Mum she said she had a headache and I could play in the garden with my kite until she felt better. But my kite blew over the fence and wouldn't come back. I didn't think she would mind me fetching it. But I thought I'd better knock on your door first. Next week I start school here, I

130

had chicken spots when we moved in so I've had a holiday. Why do they call them chicken spots? I didn't go near any chickens to catch the spots from."

Pauline found herself laughing and explaining how chicken pox was caught, and after having orange squash and biscuits, disentangling the kite's string and answering many more of Peter's questions, she was surprised to see it was nearly five o'clock.

"Come along, young man, let's take you home." So leaving a note for Bob in case he came home before she got back, they went next door with Peter carrying his kite. He rushed into his home and upstairs as fast as he could go. A woman's voice spoke and footsteps sounded on the floor above, heading for the stairs.

Hilary Stevens held out her hand to Pauline. "I'm pleased to meet you, and very sorry if Peter has been a bother. I had such a headache and he promised not to leave the garden. I won't make the mistake of leaving him alone again."

After assuring Hilary that Peter had been no trouble, Pauline turned to go.

"Can I come and see you again tomorrow?" Peter asked.

Before his mother had time to say anything, Pauline found herself saying "Yes," and then adding, "You can bring your Mummy as well if you want to." So it was settled for the morrow.

She got back home just before Bob, and told him as she prepared tea about their new neighbour. "But I thought you didn't want to get involved with anyone, and anyway, tomorrow I have the day off, had you forgotten?"

After they had talked for a while about what to do, they decided when their neighbours came over to try to keep the visit short and then go out together afterwards. The next morning Peter was at the door before his mother had closed the gate behind her.

Peter was a little quiet at first on meeting Bob, but soon perked up and asked Bob why the man down the street had no hair, and where it had gone to anyway as he'd probably had some once. Before long, Bob and Peter were busy making paper airplanes on the kitchen table while Pauline and Hilary discussed the job situation.

It was lunch time before they realised how fast the time had flown, and Hilary asked them if they would like to visit her home in the evening to meet Tom, her husband.

The afternoon was spent very quietly, Pauline and Bob went for a walk in the local woods nearby and found each other saying, "Peter would like this," or "Peter would say that," then hurriedly changing the subject.

That evening when they went around to meet Tom, the door was opened by Peter who said to Bob, "Why are you wearing a tie? My dad only wears one for work. Is it because you are a school teacher like my dad, or are you going to a wedding, that's when he wears a tie as well?"

132

Tom was teaching the same age group as Bob at another nearby school, and in no time at all they were making comparisons about their work.

Peter was full of questions, he asked Pauline if someday when he grew up he would be able to have one of those cards you put in the machine in the wall so he could get plenty of money out to buy a car, and would she stay his friend even if she got very, very old, though he knew she was quite old now? She had told him how old she was, he told his mother in a loud stage whisper.

So the evening went on, and the time flew by, soon it was time for Peter to go to bed. He went over to Bob and Pauline before going upstairs to ask if they had caught his chicken spots. They told him they'd had chicken pox when they were small, so they would not get it again.

"That's alright then, because tomorrow is Saturday and we can all go fly my kite near the woods, you can have a turn," he beamed at them.

He had gone before they could reply but his father apologized for him, saying he was lonely and needed other company, but once he had made new friends at school Peter would be fine.

When she came downstairs after settling Peter in his room Hilary offered coffee, and explained while they were drinking it that she was having another baby, that was why she had needed to lie down the previous day, she had felt queasy and had a headache.

While Bob and Tom talked about schools and pupils, Hilary talked about babies with Pauline. And Pauline began to feel something she had vowed would never affect her. A longing. A sudden need to talk of how she felt, her hopes for the future and the very new desire to have her own child. As she looked over at Bob and he caught her gaze, she knew he too was looking at life in a new light.

A voice broke into her thoughts, "Pauline, I still like you even if you are old! And anyway, you haven't lost your hair like the man down the road, so he is even older than you! But I just came down to say, *see you tomorrow!*" And Peter happily galloped back upstairs leaving his family and their guests to their laughter.

The End

One Special Day

A little girl has a special day out and meets some tiny out of this world new friends.

This is a short story to read to children.

The sun was shining, it was going to be very good weather today. Casey jumped up and down, she was so happy.

"Now, honey, stop getting so excited." Her mummy laughed as she packed the food ready for the picnic.

"But, Mummy, what if the sun gets tired and goes away, or if the clouds put a cover over the sun then we won't be able to go!"

"It's going to be nice all day, I checked the weather forecast this morning, the sun will shine for us and we will have a great time." Her mummy put more and more food into the bags that were nearly full. "Honey, go and see if Daddy is ready yet, he's outside cleaning the car and I'm nearly ready."

So Casey ran outside to her daddy who was just putting a blanket in the car. "Hello, my little ray of sunshine, you asked for good weather today, didn't you?"

Casey giggled, Daddy always called her that, "No, I didn't ask, but Mummy did and she says it's going to be really nice weather today! Daddy, are you ready yet?"

"Sure, tell Mummy I'm all set to go," her daddy replied.

So they went up into the hills behind the town where they lived, it was very pretty, lots of trees, flowers and birds were there. Soon they stopped, and Daddy spread the blanket on the ground for them to sit on while Mummy organized the picnic. Casey and her

136

daddy played games for a while, and then her mummy called them to have something to eat.

"I can catch better now, the ball doesn't fall through my fingers all the time," Casey told her mummy.

They all had plenty to eat and drink and then Casey asked her mummy if she would play with her, but Mummy thought it better for them all to rest for a while first.

"Can I pick some flowers for you then? There are a lot here, Mummy."

"All right, Casey, but stay nearby. I will be watching you all the time, don't wander away will you, honey, or I shall have to keep you right here."

Casey promised. She knew that children got lost if they went too far away, and she knew what a promise was. Her mummy had made a cake for Daddy's birthday and Casey had promised not to tell him, and she hadn't. How surprised he had been, and how proud her mummy had been when she had said 'Good girl for keeping a promise.'

Now Daddy was lying down and resting, and her mummy was watching her, so she settled down on the grass just a little way from them and began to pick flowers.

A voice made her jump. "Please put me down!" Casey looked around and saw no one. But the voice came again. *"Please put me down!"*

Looking at the flowers in her hand she saw that they were moving. There among the flowers was the prettiest little girl she had ever seen. But so tiny, and she had wings! Gently, Casey put the fairy on the grass. "I am sorry, I didn't see you there!"

"Well, I should not have been so close to people, I knew you were here but I fell asleep instead of flying away. But you didn't hurt me, your hands are quite soft. Who are you?"

"My name is Casey, I am five years old, and that is my mummy and daddy, we came here for a picnic today and we live in the town at the bottom of the hill. What is your name? Are you really a fairy? My mummy has read stories to me about you," Casey stopped for a breath.

"My name is Sunbeam, I live near here and so do lots of my family, we work here too."

"What kind of work do you do?" asked Casey.

"We make sure there is plenty of pollen for the bees, that the dew settles into upturned leaves, that the birds remember to sing, and the flowers wake up in the morning to turn their faces to the sun. There are lots of things we do, Casey. Do you want to see the rest of my family? They are working nearby."

"Yes, please. Oh, but my mummy asked me not to move away from here and I promised not to."

"You don't have to move away, just stand up, turn around and then sit down facing the other way."

Casey did as Sunbeam asked, her mummy watched and waved.

"Now look in front of you, Casey," said Sunbeam.

Casey could not believe her eyes, there were so many fairies everywhere. Some were opening petals on flowers, some were lying on blades of grass, and some were rolling up a spider's web into a ball, while others were picking up leaves from the ground that had fallen from the trees and putting them into a pile. Casey couldn't help laughing at the sight of two tiny fairies struggling to carry a large leaf between the two of them.

"Now, Casey, you see how hard the fairies are working, did you think they did so much work?"

"No, I thought that you just flew about looking pretty all the time, that's all," said Casey.

"Well, we do have fun too, watch this!" Sunbeam clapped her hands and all the fairies gathered around the hollow tree that was their home. Sunbeam spoke to them and they all looked at Casey, some flying up to settle on her shoulders.

Then the fun began, they danced, they played games, and how they laughed! "Can't catch me, can't catch me!" someone called as another fairy with her eyes closed tried to do so. "Jump, jump!" said others as they played leap-frog, some bending over while others tried to jump over them. "Catch, catch!" The tiniest ball was thrown among a group in a circle. "Skip, skip!" was called as two fairies turned a piece of a spider's web like a rope for others to skip with. Casey was giggling as she watched. Her mummy nearby smiled, she was glad they had come on this picnic, Casey was obviously enjoying sitting amongst the flowers.

But that was not all Casey sat amongst, the fairies were all around her, they formed a circle and she was in the middle of a real fairy ring. They sang as they danced around her, it was lovely music, the words came floating up to her as they danced and how pretty they all were with their wings fluttering.

The names floated on the air like whispers, such lovely names too, Silver Wisp, White Wings, Bluebell, Flower Dell, the names were pretty just like the fairies themselves, so many of them, and all so nice.

They gave her a silver thread from a jacket one of them wore, a tiny leaf, a button, and Sunbeam gave her a silver and gold flower. "Keep this always, Casey, and if you come again bring it with you, everyone here will know you are a friend of the fairies. Now after one more song you must go, but remember us and please be careful near the flowers in future."

Sunbeam joined the others in the circle as they danced and sang, it was so nice, the words came clearly to Casey:

Fairy friends this special day

All around you now we say,

A magic shake of fairy dust,
140

For our new friend is a must,

We scatter now this magic spell,

To wish you luck and wish you well.

The next thing Casey knew she was in the car. "Hi, sweetie, you fell asleep among the flowers." Her mother was holding her. Casey blinked and looked around, yes, she was on her way home and Daddy was driving the car.

But what was that in her pocket? She pulled out of her dress pocket the tiny leaf, a tiny button, a piece of silver thread and the lovely silver and gold flower. No, it had not been a dream, it was real!

Mummy was talking to Daddy; she cuddled up to her mummy and smiled, because she knew that her parents would take her back again soon so that she could have another special day with the fairies.

The End

Take a Chance

A young woman stuck in a repetitive factory job takes a chance on a new line of work, which leads to a new opportunity in her personal life.

Factory work, how she hated it! Working in a factory day after day, standing at her machine turning out leather pieces that would become a part of shoes.

Helen was bored. This job was so routine you could do it automatically. Piece after piece of leather slipped from her hands into the machine to be perforated and then dropped into a box on the other side. The box would be collected when full by Gerald, the runner, who quickly replaced it with an empty box ready for the next batch.

Helen was twenty-three; she had worked in the factory for four years now, ever since she had lost her last job when the firm had closed down. Jobs were hard to find in the town where she lived. There was no big industry, just a few minor ones that kept the town ticking over.

How glad she had been to get work, Helen recalled, so many people were unemployed and she knew she should be grateful. But five days a week doing a tedious monotonous job does not help to make one feel grateful.

She lived with her parents and her sister in a small house which was a bus ride away from where she worked. Her sister of fifteen years was still at school, her father worked at a garage repairing cars, while her mother was on the home help service working four mornings a week.

144

Really, she had a lot to be grateful for. A nice family, a good home, but oh, *this job*, how she wished she had something more interesting. Brushing her shiny brown hair back from her forehead Helen carried on churning out the pieces from her machine.

I suppose I'm not bad looking, clear complexion, good hair, blue eyes, slim, yet no boyfriend. So what is wrong with me? she wondered. But really, she knew the answer. Firstly, she would not entertain any of the brash young men who worked in the factory; secondly, there was nowhere to meet young men in her area except night clubs or public houses, places Helen had no desire to go to. And thirdly, even her mother said she was a stick in the mud, only going to places she had gone to for years, always afraid of any new challenges. Well, today she would take anything different to bring something into her life that was not the same old routine, thought Helen.

At last it was time to go home, to another evening of watching television or talking with the family. But her father had something special to say tonight.

"Helen, the garage I work for is starting a car hire firm and they want a young lady to run the office side of things, so I put your name forward, you are always complaining about wanting to leave the factory," her father said.

"But, Dad, *I daren't!* I could not take the responsibility, I just couldn't do it," answered Helen.

"Well, don't ever tell me how you hate working in the factory again. I have put your name forward and if you want it you have an interview at ten o'clock in the morning," And so saying her father settled down with his newspaper.

Helen thought over her father's words. He was right. It was the chance she needed, and she *was* always complaining about her factory work. The next morning she had decided. She took the day off for the interview, which went quite well, and her prospective new employer Mr. Jones was very nice.

When her father came home that evening he told her the job was hers, she could start in two weeks time when she had served her notice at the factory, and when the firm had completed preparations for the new car hire business. All the preliminaries were over but delivery of the cars for hiring out had to be finalised.

So came the day that Helen began her new job. It was strange and exciting, yet nerve wracking too as she learned how to handle the paperwork and talk to people both in person and over the telephone. But after her first day Helen knew she had made the right choice, it was different and certainly not boring, her father had popped across to the office at lunch time to have a quick word, and Helen went home that night feeling happier than she had for a long time.

As the days passed by she became busier as the car hire

firm became better known, and she met a large assortment of people, there was no more being bored at work.

One day Mr. Jones came in. "Helen, do you think you could fetch a car back for me? I know you have your driving license but no car of your own yet, my men are all tied up and this car has been left by a client at the airport. It's only thirty-five miles from here, you can get a bus directly there. I wouldn't normally ask but as I said, my men are all tied up," said Mr. Jones.

Well, she had said at the interview she would collect cars if necessary, so what could she do but agree? So she found herself on the bus to the airport, well, it was certainly better than being in the factory.

When she arrived at the airport, she found the car with no trouble at all, and was about to put the key in the lock when a voice made her jump.

"Just a minute, young lady! What are you doing?" It was an airport security officer, a young good looking man in uniform.

"I am taking this car back to the car hire firm I work for," answered Helen.

"Have you any proof of identity on you?" asked the young man.

Fortunately she had, so Helen produced the proof of who she was and for whom she worked.

"I am sorry to bother you but I do have my job to do," the security guard apologized.

"I understand, but I must get home or my family will worry," Helen smiled.

"My name is Steven Barnes, it was nice talking to you. Perhaps I will see you again?" he said.

"Well, maybe. But I don't usually pick up cars for my firm, this was a one-off occasion really, my name is Helen Deane, now I really must go, goodbye, Mr. Barnes."

Helen got into the car and drove away, aware that the young man was watching her as she did so.

The next day as she sat at her desk, Helen found herself thinking of the young man at the airport. He had been nice, brown hair and eyes, a nice smile, fairly tall… what am I doing? she thought. I probably won't ever see him again.

But three weeks later, Mr. Jones again called on Helen to go to the airport, and she realised as she sat on the bus that her thoughts were on Steven Barnes. I may not even see him, this is silly, she thought, but her heart beat faster as she walked across the airport car park.

Then a voice behind her said, "Hello there, Miss Deane, I have been hoping that you would come back again." It was the security guard she had been thinking of.

"Well, hello yourself! Yes, I am here to collect another car, do you want to see my papers again?" Helen teased.

"No, of course not, but I would like to talk to you if you can spare a few minutes before you go?" he answered.

Helen felt her heart thumping, this was ridiculous, she had only met this young man twice. "Well, I must not be long, what did you want to say?" Helen asked him.

"You haven't any rings on, so I am hoping you're not attached. I was wondering if I could see you sometime?" Steven asked.

"That won't be easy as we live so far apart. What did you have in mind? And please call me Helen."

"Well, Helen, may I come down to where you live this weekend and take you out?" asked Steven.

So they arranged to meet on Sunday when both of them would be free, and a smiling Helen said goodbye. It was hard to concentrate on the drive back as the picture of a pair of sparkling brown eyes kept filtering through her mind.

The days passed and Sunday arrived, she prepared to go to meet Steven with a mixture of excitement and nervousness. But after the initial greetings they were very comfortable together and chatted away quite easily. All too soon it was time for Steven to go, they said a rather sad farewell as they made arrangements to meet the following week.

As she prepared for bed that night, Helen reflected on how her life had changed since she had left the factory, now she had a job she enjoyed doing and a young man in her life!

The following Sunday they met again, and this time Helen took Steven to meet her parents and sister. He told them he lived with his widowed mother not far from the airport, his father had died when he was small and he had no brothers or sisters. Her parents were quite friendly towards him and time flew by quickly, soon it was time to part again.

Helen wondered how long they could keep up only seeing each other once a week, she knew Steven, like herself, wanted it to be more often.

The car hire firm was now quite busy and Helen found she was kept on her toes all the time booking out cars and arranging for cars to be collected when left by clients.

One day she phoned Steven as pre-arranged, but he was not at home. Puzzled, Helen said she would phone again the following night. All the next day her mind was in turmoil, there had been no word from Steven and she could hardly wait to ring him again. This time he was home, but very evasive when she asked where he had been the night before, though he quickly made arrangements to meet Helen the following weekend.

Doubts and fears made Helen's imagination run riot. Had Steven found someone else nearer home? Was he going to tell her it was all over when they met each other at the weekend? She realised just how much Steven had come to mean to her and her heart sank. But when they met Steven did not mention anything at all about the night he had been missing, and Helen was too afraid to broach the subject.

So they arranged to phone each other during the week as usual, but once again when Helen phoned Steven he was out, his mother said she would tell him Helen had called. Steven did not ring her back and time dragged by until the weekend.

When they met, Steven again said nothing about it, but this time Helen felt she must speak out. "Steven, where were you when I phoned? I was worried about you. Is everything alright?" she asked.

Steven was evasive, he apologized for not being there to answer her phone call but did not say where he had been and quickly changed the subject. This made things worse, and after Steven had gone, Helen was tormented by doubts and fears. Should she break it off with Steven before she got hurt any further? Should she demand to know what he was doing, or should she just carry on and hope it would all work out in the end?

After much thought, Helen knew she could not let it go on as if nothing was happening, nor had she the right to demand an explanation, but she also knew that she loved Steven, so how could she break it off with him? So it was with shaking hands that she dialled Steven's number in the middle of the week, and when he answered she breathed a sigh of relief.

The next evening, feeling relaxed and happy again, Helen decided to surprise Steven by phoning him. His mother told her he was out, she did not know where, and again the doubts and fears came back. The weekend visit was not as pleasant as usual and Helen knew it was her fault, she felt tense and unhappy and it showed. But when Steven asked her what was wrong, she told him it was a headache.

Now Helen was afraid to phone Steven. How she wished she had the courage to tell him it was all over between them, but she cared for him so very much. What was she to do?

Plucking up her courage she phoned as arranged and when his mother answered her heart sank.

"Hold on, Helen, here he is now," she said.

To Helen's relief Steven came on the line, but where he had been he did not say, and again Helen was too afraid to ask.

When they met at the weekend Steven seemed very excited and chattered away non-stop. Then after dinner he said, "Helen, would you come with me? I have something to show you." Leading her by the hand they headed a few streets away from Helen's own home and came to a stop before a house that was standing empty. Steven produced keys from his pocket and went inside the house followed by Helen.

"I have been coming over here secretly, trying to finalise things with the owner of this house who has now moved out. My mother and I are moving in here, Helen, I can't bear being apart from you, yet could not leave my mother on her own, she hates living near the airport and is delighted to be coming here. Also I have a new job as a security guard here in town at a local bank, so very soon now we can be together much more. I did not want to say anything just in case these plans did not work out, but come and look around the house now."

Helen was speechless, all the bad things she had been thinking, yet he had only been thinking of how to get closer to her. They walked around the house, Helen giving it her approval, and then returned to Helen's home where she was surprised to find that her family had been in on the secret. Her mother had met Mrs. Barnes and gone to the new house with her, then taken her home for tea. It was clear that the two women had got on quite well together.

Her father chuckled as he told her how he had been putting Steven in touch with any jobs that he heard of in town, and her younger sister just said she thought Steven was 'dishy'!

How lucky can you be? thought Helen as she looked around at her family and Steven, everything has become so right for me, to think if I had not changed my job none of this would have happened.

Thank goodness I found the willpower to take a chance!

The End

One by Another

A petulant young woman marches out of a village dance and has a life changing experience.

Marvellous isn't it! thought Mary in annoyance, everyone else gets a lift home but just because I was mad at Jeff and I walked out, now everyone has gone and I find myself here alone! She looked around at the village hall where the dance had been held, if only she lived here in Soby and not in the next village two miles away! Everywhere was quiet, there was not a soul about except herself. She reflected on the evening and how she had come to be standing here alone.

How delighted she had been when Jeff had asked her to go to the Soby village dance, it was a slightly larger village than Kirkham where she and Jeff lived and therefore had more events than their own village, albeit few compared with town life, but the nearest town was a long way off. Really, Mary thought crossly, it's all Jeff's fault! I should have known, men are such fickle creatures, a pretty face and they behave in such a stupid manner.

When Jeff had first broached the subject of going to the village dance and his hopes of taking Mary, it had all seemed so good. Deciding what to wear, promising to her parents to be home before midnight, and excitement at the thought of dancing while held tightly in Jeff's arms.

She had grown up with Jeff, they'd gone to the same schools, played games together, and she'd lived within a stone's throw of the young man who had always been a big part of her life.

When they were children wherever Jeff was, Mary was not far behind, often to his acute embarrassment.

Mary thought back over the years as she stood alone in the dark, letting her mind wander to the picnic she had been to only three weeks before. She had gone with a group of friends which of course included Jeff, they had all gone over to Highgate Farm where they had found a place to set up the picnic.

After eating and drinking, the fun began, playing silly games together, climbing trees, behaving like children all over again, and finally the pairing off of couples as they all wandered away from the picnic area for a stroll before going back home.

Mary and Jeff had paired off together, and they'd wandered among the trees of a small wood near the picnic area, not speaking for a while, but content to just be together. It was after walking in silence for a while that Jeff had mentioned the upcoming dance to Mary. Having already heard about the dance, Mary was delighted that Jeff wanted to take her and agreed that she would love to go.

The rest of the afternoon had sped by, walking, talking, laughing together, Mary could not imagine life without Jeff as part of it, they were a pair. Everyone knew they belonged together. Just three days after the picnic it happened—the people next door to Jeff's family had a visitor.

She was, it seemed, the niece of Mrs. Foster, and she had been abroad with her parents since being a toddler, but now as a young woman she had decided she wanted to see her native England. Therefore she had written from Australia to her aunt asking if she could stay for a three month visit.

Now Lauren was here, and how heads had turned to stare at her! Not that she was a raving beauty, but she had a certain poise and style of her own that made everyone notice her. Jeff of course was introduced as he lived next door to her aunt, and from then on Mary had seen the change in Jeff.

It was all 'Lauren said' or 'Lauren did', until Mary felt she could scream. She knew it was irrational and childish, after all, it was only for three months, but fear made her imagination run riot. What if Jeff had fallen for Lauren? What if he went back to Australia with her, or she stayed here in England and they married and settled down in the village? Mary felt that she could not bear the thought of such a thing happening, but what could she do?

Over the next week she saw less and less of Jeff, and when she did, all he could talk about was Lauren. The final blow was when he said to her, "You don't mind if I escort Lauren to the dance, do you? I know Don wants you to go with him, and I really feel obliged to take Lauren as she is my neighbour."

Mary was furious, it was true Don Hanson had begged to take her to the dance, and although he was a nice young man, he wasn't Jeff. But she could not scream and shout in fury as she felt like doing. So holding her feelings in check she agreed, especially as Jeff had promised to be with her when they arrived at the dance.

The evening of the dance came, and Mary had gone with Don while Jeff escorted Lauren, and for a while it all seemed to go well. Lauren had a lot of admirers, so was quickly whisked off to dance. Jeff danced with Mary, and Don went to get himself a drink. Before the evening was half over with however, it had all changed. Jeff and Lauren were together for almost every dance, and when they were not dancing they were laughing and chatting as if they had known each other for years.

Watching them closely, Mary paid little attention to poor Don, who was trying very hard to please her, fetching drinks and food, offering every dance to her and chatting away about all kinds of things. But it was no use, Mary was so overwhelmed by jealousy nothing else penetrated her mind, so while Don had gone to fetch another drink for her she collected her coat and rushed outside.

Wandering through the village, she didn't know what she was doing or where she was heading, it was no use trying to go home, her mother would want to know why, and anyway, Don had brought her in his car. Two miles may not be much to walk in daylight, but it was now dark, and the lane leading to her own village was not an inviting prospect. In the sunshine with the fields on each side it was very nice, a pleasant stroll from Soby to Kirkham, but now the prospect of walking alone in the dark did not appeal to Mary at all.

So she wandered along the main village street and thought about Lauren and Jeff. Why had she come to spoil things? Everyone knew that Mary and Jeff were meant for each other, right from being children everyone had known, and now that Mary was eighteen and Jeff twenty, all the village knew they were serious about each other, but now it was spoilt because of the visitor from Australia.

Mary turned off the main street and wandered along a quiet side street where rows of cottages stood, as she went further along the street she became aware of an elderly lady shuffling along in front of her. Catching up with her, Mary was about to go past when the lady spoke.

"Excuse me, dear, could you give me your arm? It isn't far, but I'm not as young as I used to be and my poor old body is not as willing as my mind."

Mary quickly proffered her arm to the stranger and fell in step beside her. "Where are you going?" she asked.

"Not much further, my dear. The last cottage down this street is where I live; perhaps you will come in for a few minutes? I live alone you see, so despite the late hour no one will be disturbed," said the lady.

Mary decided she would go in for a while, after all they would not be going home from the dance for some time yet, and she did not want to get back too soon and find Jeff and Lauren still

160

together.

So they came to the end cottage and the lady took out a key from her pocket, unlocking the door they stepped inside.

Mary was surprised when the light came on to see that it looked quite dowdy, and not really 'lived-in' at all, but her attention was taken by the lady talking to her.

"Now, my dear, sit down for a while and rest. What were you doing wandering about on your own tonight?" she asked.

To her surprise Mary found herself explaining why she was not at the dance, and when she was finished she sat quietly waiting for a reaction.

"Well, my dear, jealousy is not a nice emotion. It can destroy all the finer feelings one has you know, and hide the truth from you if you let it mask everything. Try to look at it in a logical manner. What has your young man done? Shown attention to this young lady? Well, don't you think he probably had some pressure from his parents? After all, they are very good friends of Lauren's aunt. I feel sure they would have discussed her stay here with Jeff and his parents. Also, what if the position was reversed and it was you with a young man visiting here, do you think Jeff would have been so dogmatic?"

The lady looked at Mary as she spoke. Mary was quiet, thinking. Yes, Jeff's parents were great friends of Mrs. Foster, and it was indeed likely they had asked for help with Lauren. Also if she had been in Jeff's place and it was a young man in Lauren's place, then she knew Jeff would have offered to help in any way, and not resented her being away from him.

"Well," she said. "I'm sure you're right, but it's so difficult when you care about someone so much. How can I overcome the jealousy and help instead?"

"The only way one emotion can be controlled is by another stronger one overtaking it, so you must ask yourself how much you care, and if it means more than the jealousy you now feel," said her elderly companion.

"That's easier said than done. I feel so hurt seeing Jeff with Lauren all the time," said Mary.

"But you know it's only for a while, and she will be going home. Try to be patient and be more friendly to her, offer her a welcome while she is here, and don't let your imagination run away with you about what *might* happen. Remember, no one knows what may happen to any of us tomorrow." So saying, the old lady stood up. "Excuse me, dear, I must go upstairs for a moment." She went out of the door facing Mary and disappeared. Mary sat quietly for a while, and then began to look around her. What a strange room, it looked as if no one bothered much about it. The curtains were shabby, everywhere needed dusting and a general air of apathy hung over the whole room.

Mary felt ashamed of herself; after all, this old lady

162

obviously lived alone and was not a very healthy person. The old lady came back carrying a photograph which she handed to Mary.

"Look at this, my dear, this young man was once engaged to me but I lost him. Like you I was consumed with jealousy, not over another woman, but because Jack loved his work. He was a sailor and just wanted to carry on being a sailor, but I had to object. I wanted him to give up the sea, so in the end I gave him a choice—the sea or me. Well, he sailed away and I never saw him again."

The photograph was of a young man in naval uniform, very handsome and smart. "How very sad for you, did you never hear from him again?" asked Mary.

"Never. If only I had realised I could have shared him, then I wouldn't have lost him. You know you can't dictate, Mary, and if you love someone you must share them," the old lady had tears in her eyes as she spoke.

Mary felt ashamed of herself, yes, it was true she had dominated Jeff, and no, she had not offered her friendship to Lauren.

She sat talking with the old lady about the lost romance and time slipped by, suddenly looking at her watch, Mary realised she ought to be getting back to the dance.

"May I come and see you again sometime?" she asked her new-found friend.

"You will see me again, Mary, I'm sure," the old lady replied.

So Mary took her leave and headed back to the village hall, where to her amazement she found everywhere in darkness. So here she was, faced with getting home by herself in the dark. I suppose they thought I had rung my father to fetch me, or they would not have gone without me, she mused.

Well, there's nothing else for it, I had better get going, she decided, and began walking down the lane to her own village.

It was dark and lonely, and although she could have rung her father had he been home, she knew he was not, he had gone to visit his brother and was staying overnight in the town where her uncle lived. Her mother could not fetch her as her father had the car, and she did not want to ring her mother and worry her by saying she was walking home alone in the dark. Of course she could have rung Jeff, he was unaware her father was not at home, but shame for the way she had behaved prevented her from doing so.

So Mary kept walking, going at a steady pace, she could not help wondering why the dance had finished relatively early, it was so unusual, everyone was very reluctant to leave the dance as a rule, yet everyone had disappeared tonight. Well, tomorrow she would ask Jeff and also apologize for her childish behaviour, then she would visit Lauren and make a big effort to become her friend.

164

Other than the screech of an owl, the rustling of the trees and the sound of the little brook bubbling in the hedgerow, all was still. Before long Mary knew she had nearly arrived, she knew this road well, it was not far now, nearly home. As she saw the houses of the village take shape before her, Mary realised lights were still on in some of the homes, so some people were still up, she thought.

As she headed towards her own home a car suddenly came along the road. As it drew near she could see it was Jeff's car so she stepped closer to it and waved her arms, but Jeff never saw her and went speeding by. Well, I *thought* he would have seen me, wherever can he be going? There wasn't anyone else in the car, perhaps he has gone to look for me, but there is nothing I can do now, thought Mary.

So she came to her own gate, to see all the lights on inside and there were signs of movement through the drawn curtains. Going up the path she suddenly saw to her surprise the little old lady from Soby village standing before her.

"Hello, how did you get here?" Mary asked.

"Come, Mary, my message was too late. Do come with me," the old lady replied.

"But I must go in, my mother will be worried about me. How did you get here before me? What is happening?" Mary demanded.

"Come and let me show you before you go into your

home," said the old lady.

Mary allowed herself to be drawn away by the old lady, but then she saw Lauren and her aunt come hurrying toward them.

"Hello, I'm here! I'm sorry if I worried you!" said Mary.

To her surprise they both hurried past and went to knock on the door of Mary's home. They were quickly let in.

"Mary, come with me," again the old lady urged. "You will see in a moment, all will be revealed."

Mary again fell in step beside the old lady; they moved away from the village street and began to go back towards Soby village. Strangely, they were there in no time at all, and Mary was led to the main street. Jeff's car was parked outside the local constable's home but Jeff was not in the car.

The old woman took Mary to the cottage where she had been earlier that evening. But there was no cottage. Just a pile of rubble. "What has happened to your home?" Mary grabbed for the old woman's hand but her hand hit only air. Only a shimmering apparition stood at her side.

"I tried to help, Mary, but I was too late…"

Suddenly, before her eyes the old lady vanished. Mary stood there for a moment in utter shock, and then hurried back to where Jeff's car was parked. He was coming out of the house with the constable.

166

"I'm sorry, Jeff, but there was nothing anyone could have done, she came tearing out of the dance and ran straight in front of farmer Gibson's truck. Such a pretty girl, such a shame," the constable said shaking his head sadly.

"It was my fault," said Jeff, "I should have been taking care of her, paying her more attention. Why did she go off in such a hurry though? And you know, constable, strangely enough, when I was coming over here, just for a moment I thought I saw Mary near her home."

"Now, lad, don't let your imagination play tricks on you. It's because you were thinking about her, that's all," said the constable.

Looking at Jeff's tear stained face Mary knew she had lost, lost what might have been, and as she felt herself fading the constable's words came to her.

"Funny thing is, lad, you know old Miss Tate who lived around the corner? Her cottage has long since fallen down, but Don swears he saw her ghost right near the accident."

"You know for a while we thought Mary was going to make it when they got her to the hospital. But it wasn't to be, lad, it wasn't to be."

"But I'm here! *I'm right here*!" Mary cried.

A firm hand clamped down on her shoulder, she turned to look but there was no one there. Then suddenly the hand began to shake her very gently but firmly.

"Mary, lass! Wake up!"

Mary opened her eyes to find Jeff's concerned features close to her own. She looked around—she was still at the dance! She flung her arms around him, holding him tight. He chuckled, dropping a light kiss on her cheek.

"You were dreaming, talking in your sleep, too!"

"I must have been exhausted."

"You must have been, to fall asleep here with all the noise going on!"

Mary looked around, she'd thought about leaving the dance but had instead sat down in the corner feeling a little out of sorts and a bit sulky, then she'd closed her eyes and fallen asleep. She looked across the room, Lauren was dancing with Don, Jeff held his hand out.

"Want to dance?"

"I'd love to."

Mary stepped into Jeff's warm and comforting arms. "I was thinking, perhaps I could invite Lauren to go shopping with me tomorrow?"

"I'm sure she'd love that," Jeff said with a smile.

Mary rested her cheek against Jeff's shoulder, not entirely

168

surprised to see a vague shimmering shape of an older woman drift past the window, and sighed in contentment at her second chance.

The End

Grey Day

A quiet elderly gentleman gives would-be robbers exactly what they deserve, and it's the last thing they expect.

The mist came slipping in over the beach, across the promenade and silently passed over the road and houses to hang in the air, cold and silent.

Only hours before there had been no sign of the change to come, a grey day, and yet there had been the promise of the sun breaking through. How different everything looked now, how strange.

The house that was only yards from the promenade was rather like the mist, grey, strange and silent. Just like the man who lived there alone, since his wife had died many years ago, no children, only a few choice friends, and little contact with people.

He sat looking out of the window but could not really see much at all, just the mist, he sighed and turned back to what he was doing, a stamp collection of many years was in the room, and he was busy sorting out yet more stamps.

A knock on the door made him jump, he hesitated, decided to ignore it and carried on. But the knock became insistent, sighing he made his way to the door, none of his friends ever called unannounced, only people promoting their religion or collectors for charity. Pulling open the door he saw a young man and woman there, sure enough she had a collecting box, smiling they asked for a donation, he shook his head and began to close the door.

Suddenly the smiles had gone, the young man grabbed him,

172

pushing him backwards and the woman slammed the door after them as they all filled the narrow hallway.

"Right, we know you have a stamp collection worth a lot of money, we want it and anything else you have of value here," the young man barked.

He was pushed into the room where the fire glowed brightly. Their eyes lit up at the sight of the stamps, but first they had to deal with the grey man.

"Fell for it, didn't you!" the woman jeered. "We stole this box from a local shop so that we could use it as a prop." The woman jingled the box before putting it down on the table.

The grey man sat down, he should have known better than to open his door to unexpected visitors, usually he had more sense. "How did you know about my collection?" he asked.

"Never mind how, we do, so just stay still then you won't get hurt," the young man sniggered.

They began to gather a lifetime of his hobby together, opening drawers, piling it up, and almost ignoring him as they did so. The woman went upstairs and was gone for a while, the young man kept an eye on his victim as he went on opening cupboards, pulling books from the bookcase and searching for any hidden items of value.

Carrying two suitcases the woman returned, she opened one of the cases and showed the young man some money, ornaments, and a velvet case. "These were up there in the bedroom; we can put everything we want in the cases to take with us."

They began to put the collection into the suitcases, leaving the velvet case on one side for a moment. It was at the sight of this that the grey man changed and did not look quite so grey anymore. A gleam had appeared in his eyes. He began to clench his fists and tighten his jaw.

The couple could have been in their own home, they chatted away together seeming relaxed at how easy it had all been for them. After all, they knew where to sell the stuff, and thanks to the window cleaner who had talked about this man's collection in the local tavern on the seafront where they had stopped for a drink, they were laughing.

"Well, old man, we are going now, if you are sensible you won't go out or call for help, we know you don't have a phone here, remember we can always come back if you talk, so be a good boy and forget we came," the man said in a sing-song patronizing tone.

With a roar the grey man flew from his chair. First he headed for the young man who was so startled he moved back, but not quickly enough, the grey man's feet flew through the air hitting the young man in the chest, down he went. Before he could get up, the grey man was at him, pulling him up by the arm he flung him across the room, the woman was staring in horror, but the grey man had not finished yet. He grabbed the young man around the neck, pulling his arms behind his back and at the same time forced his former bully to his knees. Swiftly he snapped a pair of handcuffs on him and pushed him into a chair.

The young man's eyes were bulging with fear, he gasped for breath as the grey man turned to look for the young woman, she made a dash for the door. But not quickly enough. He held her in an iron grip.

"You're breaking my arm!" she yelled.

Tossing her into a second chair the grey man looked at them.

"If you had not tried to take my medals I may not have got so angry." He picked up the velvet case from where it had fallen in the chaos. "I worked in Hong Kong for many years and they taught me a lot. How to defend myself, how to be discreet and live my life quietly, how to make the best of my collection and add to it, and how to accept my life as it is. When you came here and lied, forcing your way in, I was almost ready to accept, but you see, my medals are for other qualities during my life in the army." He opened the velvet case and there was a row of shining medals.

"Now, we must do something about you two, mustn't we?" He pulled the young man from his chair, the woman stood up too, looking pale and scared.

He tied a cord around the woman's wrists while the young

man watched fearfully, and then led them from the house into his garden and down to a big shed. There he locked them in among the potato sacks, plant pots and garden tools.

As he walked back to the house he smiled, one part of his training he had forgotten— always be on your guard. Well now he would pay for that by having the police ask questions, and his peace would be disturbed again.

He headed for the public telephone box noting that the mist had lifted just for a short while, and the passage of time had also lifted for the grey man.

The End

So Ordinary

A lonely widow finds new friends thanks to a persistent furry visitor.

She wandered down the garden path looking straight in front of her. Would it be there? Every day for the past week it had been at the bottom of the garden.

She supposed it had jumped over the wall. But why did it keep coming back? Had it no home to go to? Yet it looked well cared for.

The spaniel was sitting next to the blackcurrant bush and as she approached it looked at her with its limpid soulful eyes. There was something about those eyes which made it hard to resist their owner.

Agnes Telford was no exception, from the first day she had come down the garden to find the dog there she had been unable to resist. She had made a half-hearted attempt to shoo the dog away, but not really trying to get rid of it. And now each day she hurried out to look for her new friend who always waited at the bottom of the garden and would not follow her into the house, no matter how she tried to coax it.

The trouble was that she was getting too fond of Suzy as she had called the dog. Living alone and having no visitors had never bothered her before, in fact she preferred it that way, always being a loner since her husband had died.

They had moved to this retirement cottage full of dreams of how they would spend their later years. Nine months later Harry

Telford had died from a heart attack, leaving his widow feeling bitter and angry at life. She had made no attempt to get to know anyone, and made a once weekly trip for her shopping to the local store, keeping herself aloof from everyone.

Then had come the day when she wandered into her garden and found the dog, Agnes Telford was now a different person, buying treats for the dog on her last shopping trip had made it seem a brighter day.

The dog sniffed at Agnes's hand as she reached out, and then sat patiently as she was petted. There was a rapport between the woman and the dog that was unmistakable.

Agnes sat on the seat her husband had made for the garden and Suzy sat at her feet.

A feeling of contentment filled Agnes, one thing she was careful about was the garden, it had been Harry's pride and joy after years of living in a town, he had nurtured the garden and tended it with loving care.

Feeling that she was doing it for Harry, the garden was also well kept by Agnes, and when she finished gardening she would sit on this seat to survey her private domain. But having someone to share it with made it seem even better. It was as if Suzy knew, she never walked on the flower borders and appeared to pick her way around the garden most carefully.

Who could Suzy belong to? And why was she not missed?

Agnes could not help but wonder, yet she felt she did not want to know really, after all, Suzy's owner would surely stop her visits to Agnes's garden.

So as the afternoon wore on, Suzy had a drink of water and a dog biscuit, Agnes had a cup of tea, then as if by a pre-arranged signal Suzy got up and shook herself and walked away.

Agnes knew she would not come back again today, she always did the same thing each day.

After she had gone, Agnes went into the cottage and busied herself but her mind was on tomorrow and Suzy's visit.

The next day she was ready and waiting, but no dog appeared. Fearfully Agnes sat on the garden seat watching out for Suzy. After an hour she realised it was hopeless. So, the owner had stopped the dog from roaming? It was what she had expected wasn't it? So why did she feel so let down? Getting up, Agnes went indoors, well she might as well forget the dog now. The old bitter expression settled on her face as she set about doing the ironing.

She had just finished it when there was a knock at the door. Agnes never had visitors, she discouraged any contact with people, so frowning she went to answer the summons at the door.

A little lady with white hair stood there and on a lead was Suzy. Agnes's face lit up at the sight of the dog before she could stop herself.

180

"It is you then, Mrs. Telford, I knew she was going somewhere! Well, today I followed her and put her on the lead as she was about to go into your garden. My name is Hilda Sansom, I live down the lane from you. She is such a dear and she seems to have taken to you, don't you, Tina?" The lady bent down to pat the dog who looked from one to the other with soulful eyes.

"You had better come in, Mrs. Sansom," said Agnes, standing back to allow her visitor room.

They went into the cosy sitting room and sat down, Tina sat on the floor between them, her head on her paws.

"I knew she must belong to someone, she is obviously very well cared for but she came every afternoon and kept me company. I did not know what to do," said Agnes.

"Please don't worry, I don't mind at all. You see I am on my own too, and I know what Tina means to me since my husband died two years ago, I don't know what I would have done without her. But I don't mind sharing her, really I don't. And please call me Hilda," said Mrs. Samson.

Before long they were chatting away as if they had known each other for years. Hilda telling Agnes how her husband had died from a stroke, and how they had lived in the village for five years, and that her children were married, one living in Australia and one living in London.

Agnes related how she'd been unable to have any children,

that she and her husband had been everything to each other and how devastated she was when he died.

After a cup of tea together the two women decided to see each other again, and if Tina was missing, Hilda would come to Agnes for her. So it was with a light heart and a contented smile that Agnes saw Hilda and Tina leave.

The following weeks were busy ones, they went shopping together, had coffee, exchanged recipes and became good friends. Tina accepted the situation readily and would go and sit in Agnes's garden while they were talking or lie on the floor between them.

Then came the day when Hilda came hurrying round to Agnes looking for Tina, but she was not there, nor could they find her anywhere. By evening they were getting really worried, no Tina appeared that night at all.

The next day Agnes detected a note of coolness in her new friend when they met, but could not understand why.

Hilda reported Tina missing to the police and again went searching for her. After a while Agnes asked her to join her for a cup of tea while they gathered themselves again.

Over the tea Agnes asked Hilda what was wrong, and was shocked when she replied, "If I had not been so silly in letting Tina visit you this would not have happened. I know how fond of her you are; you aren't hiding her, are you?"

Agnes was shocked and hurt, then angry. Heated words
182

followed and Hilda left with Agnes's words ringing in her ears, vowing never to return. "I should never have trusted anyone!"

So for two more days the search went on for Tina, the police said someone must have taken her away by car, which was not very comforting.

Agnes and Hilda remained apart with Agnes going back to her tight unsmiling expression again.

On the fourth day of Tina's disappearance, Agnes was in her garden weeding. She looked up on hearing a noise and saw Tina being held on a leash by a frail looking old gentleman.

"What are you doing with that dog?" she exclaimed hurrying toward the pair.

"Please may I sit down? I still feel so weak," he said.

He sat beside her on the garden bench and introduced himself as Albert Walters and began to explain. He had felt unwell a few days ago while out in his garden and had noticed the dog there just looking at him. He lived alone, and going into his house he laid down on the sofa. He had got worse and was unable to go upstairs to bed, but every time he had opened his eyes the dog was there, looking at him and licking his hand as if to encourage him.

Gradually he had felt a little better and staggered into the kitchen to feed himself and the dog who'd had nothing to eat while he was ill. Then at last he had found the strength to walk and wanted to return the dog to its owner and say how wonderful she was. Tina had led him here.

Agnes listened quietly while stroking Tina, then she said, "Well, she is not my dog but I will ring her owner for you, rest here a moment."

Going inside she rang Hilda and told her what had occurred, there was silence on the other end of the phone for a minute, and then Hilda said she would be there at once.

Agnes made some tea and set out a plate of biscuits, and also a bowl of water and dog biscuits for Tina.

When Hilda arrived she poured the tea and let Albert tell Hilda the story. When he had finished, Hilda looked at Agnes shame-faced. "I am sorry, Agnes. I should have known. Tina has such a big heart and she senses when someone needs her. How could I have said such things to you?"

Before Albert's bewildered eyes the two women were crying and laughing together. Tina went to lie at his feet as if she could not understand the fuss either.

They all chatted away together over tea and biscuits, and it soon became apparent that Albert was lonely too. It made them wonder how many older folk were alone and lonely. Hilda said, "How many times is Tina going to be the 'Good Samaritan' when really, we all ought to do something."

After inviting Albert for tea the next day, Hilda and Agnes decided they would find out how many people lived alone around

184

them, then they would invite them around to their homes. If there were too many then they would hire a hall and get a club going. Why should so many people be alone and lonely when they could change the situation?

So, full of ideas, Agnes and Hilda parted company for the night, each relieved their friendship had been repaired.

As Agnes prepared to settle for the night she could not help thinking about Tina, how strange that a dog had started all of this, just as if she knew. Agnes was sure that Tina had looked at her in a knowing manner as she patted the dog goodnight.

Yet, she was just a dog, wasn't she? An ordinary dog? No, there was nothing ordinary about Tina, she was so much more.

The End

The Joker

*The family joker and the new man in a young woman's life
discover they have something in common.*

Her Uncle Tom was a joker, a real 'card', as her mum
called him. He'd always been able to make her laugh with his
jokes, his magic tricks and his handling of a pack of cards. Jean
could hear him laughing in the kitchen with her mother, and no
doubt as his sister, her mum was giving him some advice and
encouragement.

It was only just over a year since he had lost Ava, his wife;
they had no children, so now Tom was an even more frequent
visitor to their home. Jean liked him and enjoyed his display of
tricks, that is, *she had*. But since meeting Dean a few months ago
and bringing him home, she felt torn.

The first time Dean had met her parents and Uncle Tom, he
was very polite about Uncle Tom's jokes and tricks, but she had
noticed how every time since then when her uncle got out his pack
of cards, a frown had appeared on Dean's face. She loved her uncle
but had come to realise that she loved Dean, and she dreaded the
routine weekly get-together at her home. The disapproval on
Dean's face worried her, she could not stop her uncle and hurt his
feelings, but she did not want to lose Dean either.

Saturday evening arrived when they met as usual at Jean's
home for dinner, then they would all sit talking afterwards until
Uncle Tom took over to display his latest tricks, to fool them with
his sleight of hand, or just tell them jokes. Jean's teenage brother

was out as usual, he would not be a part of what he called 'an old fogey's evening'. Her father was a quiet man, content to let Tom take over. Jean felt quite desperate, and when Uncle Tom said, "Who wants to see my latest trick?" she hurriedly said, "Let's just have a game of cards for a change, shall we?"

Although they were surprised, her parents agreed, and was that a look of relief she saw on Dean's face? The evening was quite pleasant, Dean played very well and seemed to thoroughly enjoy the games. Uncle Tom praised him and said how well he had done. The following weeks fell into a pattern; dinner first then card games, no tricks from Uncle Tom at all, and Dean seemed more relaxed than ever, even suggesting that they play for a small sum of money.

That was when Jean began to worry again. Had she fallen for a man who was a secret gambler? Did he go gambling in the evenings when they didn't see each other? To think she had stopped poor Uncle Tom's enjoyment, and for what? She was most concerned.

By the time the next Saturday evening had arrived Jean was really upset, and after dinner when they all went into the sitting room she determined to ask Uncle Tom to perform for them again, if only to see what Dean's reaction would be.

However, Tom was regaling his sister and brother-in-law with stories of when he was a carpet fitter. He told them many tales of the things that had happened to him during those years. On one occasion he was expected to move two cages of pet monkeys before he could take up the old carpet and fit the new, another time a man insisted on kneeling with him 'in case he needed any help' the entire time he was working. It made them all laugh as they imagined them kneeling side by side until the carpet was in place.

But when Tom had finished talking, Dean asked. "Shall we have a game of cards now?"

Jean jumped up, "No, let's have Uncle Tom show us some of his tricks, we haven't seen any for ages."

Dean's hurt expression made Jean look away, but Uncle Tom got out his pack of cards and said, "Well, I do have a couple of new ones to show you!" He shuffled the cards and then began to demonstrate his new tricks for them.

Dean got up from his seat and strode across the room, for a moment Jean thought he was leaving, but he went over to Uncle Tom and took the cards from him. "I can't stand it any longer, for goodness sake at least let me show you how to do it!"

He seemed to change before their eyes, and they watched in amazement as he let the cards cascade from hand to hand without a fault in a most professional manner. Then he showed them tricks with the cards that made Uncle Tom seem very slow indeed, the quickness of his hand did indeed deceive the eye as they tried to follow what Dean was doing.

190

When he stopped, Jean asked. "Where did you learn all that? I thought you didn't like watching Uncle Tom. Are you a gambler, Dean, is that why you handle the cards so well?"

Dean laughed. "The only reason I didn't appear happy when watching Uncle Tom was because I wanted to help him improve his performance. No, I am not a gambler, I am a member of the Magic Circle, and I felt frustrated at not being able to say anything when I had just started to come here, but now I feel a part of the family there is no harm in you knowing, and Tom and I can get together to go over our tricks."

There was a shout of laughter from Uncle Tom and both her parents joined in as she and Dean began to laugh. The cards which had been in Dean's hands suddenly appeared out of Uncle Tom's collar.

Oh yes, he was a 'card' alright, but now she had the full pack—including two jokers!

The End

Solly

An alien observer is sent to file a report on human behaviour and he is not impressed.

What a strange place this is, not at all what I've been used to. And all these high buildings! Why do they go up and up? Not a pretty sight, thought Solly.

Well, I've been sent here so I might as well make the most of it. Now, where was I? Oh, yes, I was going down to the big stately looking building.

Solly headed off down the street toward the city museum, walking slowly and looking around as he did so. Where I live it's all on one level and so compact, everyone can walk about in comfort, no stretching yourself to look up at a building, so much better! I'm glad that I don't live here, he thought.

The museum was open. He walked in and began to look around, pulling a notebook from his pocket he began to make notes. History was so interesting, especially how people used to live.

Walking around the museum he became engrossed in what he was doing and filled many pages of his notebook. Finally, deciding he'd had enough he walked outside, the sun was shining and people were hurrying in all directions.

Why is everyone always in a hurry here? They are always dashing about as if every second counts, I can't understand it, thought Solly.

Going down the street he headed for the park. At least there people won't be rushing about and I can sit and watch them. The park was a large one as befits a city, but there was room on a bench to sit down. Out came the notebook and pen again, and watching the people walking, talking, laughing, and enjoying the sunshine, Solly's pen flew over the pages.

A man sitting near him was watching what he was doing.

"Excuse me, do you write for a newspaper or something?" he asked. "You certainly are busy there; can I help in any way at all?"

Solly looked at the man, comparing the man's small frame with his own five feet ten inches.

The man was small and red-cheeked, with bright eyes which were a shade of green; he had sandy hair and was obviously consumed with curiosity.

Solly smiled at him. "Thank you, but I am just doing a little research. I just have to observe, that's all, so no one can help me."

"Well, just thought I would ask," said the little man.

That's the trouble here, thought Solly, everyone interferes as well. Where I live we leave others alone unless they ask for help or advice.

He closed his notebook and stood up. Well, it was time to eat now anyway, so he would have to go to get something and hopefully he'd be able to eat it in peace.

Walking across the park he looked carefully at couples walking with arms entwined, at children playing, prams being pushed by mothers, elderly residents strolling along, and dogs being led on leads by their owners.

Going out of the park he headed for a restaurant, and stepping inside he found a vacant table to sit at. Nothing on the menu appealed to him very much, but he must eat, so finally he chose a meal and ordered it. He looked around while he was waiting for his dinner to arrive, so many different types of people here, and all were either eating or chattering. Did they not know how to sit quietly? Solly thought. He was the only one who was just sitting, but of course he had no one to talk to.

No sooner had he thought this than a couple stopped by his table, they were obviously looking for somewhere to sit.

"May we join you?" the man asked, "there doesn't seem to be anywhere else to sit."

Looking around, Solly realised the restaurant had filled up, there was indeed nowhere else left for the couple. "Sit down, please do," he said, "You can share my table with pleasure." With smiling faces the couple joined him and settled down to look at the menu.

It was not long though, before the inevitable conversation began.

"Do you come here often for a meal? Is the food good? We

196

just came here for the first time today."

It was the woman who spoke. Quite a pretty young woman, curly blonde hair, blue eyes, very dainty and polite.

Solly answered her. "No, this is my first time here. I just came in for dinner."

"Do you live in the city?" the man asked him, "We live outside the city quite a way, and have just come in for the day."

So the polite conversation went on, flitting from one thing to another—and how Solly wished he was alone—but there is no way in a city you can be alone in public places.

Finally finishing his meal, he rose, and bidding his eating companions farewell he went out into the sunlight again, heading this time for the shopping centre.

Strolling among the shoppers he kept pausing to make notes in his book as he observed the actions of the people around him.

All the time the ceaseless chatter of the people to each other. Never ending sounds of gossip and information. Solly headed for one of the seats in front of the shops where he sat down and began writing in his book again.

"Hey, Mister, is that what they call shorthand?" A young girl was peering over his shoulder. Solly quickly closed his book and looked up.

"You wouldn't understand," he said.

"Well, it's funny writing anyway," the young girl replied with a shrug.

Solly stood up, never any peace wherever he went! Always someone wanting to ask questions about what he was doing.

He walked out of the shopping centre and headed towards the area where he knew the official buildings of the city were. The town hall, police station and an art gallery were first, after a moment's thought he headed for the art gallery.

Strolling around the paintings, sculptures and bronze figures he again reached for his notebook. Quickly making notes as he walked around the room, he soon had filled many pages. He sat down on one of the seats provided and scanned what he had written, yes, so far all was good, it was what was needed and he felt that he was doing a good job.

A voice made him jump. "I just love art galleries, don't you?"

It was an elderly lady who had sat down beside him, so engrossed had Solly been that he had not noticed her.

"My favourite artists are Constable and Renoir," she said. "I hate these modern artists, they are just rubbish."

Solly felt he must reply. "Well, I like a lot of artists myself and find the variations interesting."

"Yes, but you can't compare the great artists with today's so-called 'artists', can you?" she said.

"No, I don't suppose so," he replied cautiously.

Solly could see he would be trapped into a long discussion if he didn't move, so murmuring excuses he stood up and moved away into the next room.

Going around the gallery once more he made notes and was so busy that he was again surprised by a voice beside him. "Excuse me, sir, may I ask why you are writing in that book?" It was a gallery attendant.

"I am doing some research, that is all," Solly replied.

"We have to be careful here you know, though we don't have any originals, only copies, you never know what some people will do. I've heard of people noting down the amount of security guards on duty, the location of the exits and the type of alarm system used and so on, before returning to break in."

"I assure you I am not thinking of taking anything," said Solly wondering if the man had been watching too many movies.

"Alright, sir, but no more note taking please," said the attendant drawing himself up to his full height and looking stern.

Solly smiled, nodded and headed for the outer doors as the attendant strode off with his hands neatly folded behind his back.

Well, he would sit out here and watch the police station for a while. Men in blue uniforms kept going in and out as Solly sat on a low wall watching, and cars kept coming and going from behind the building too.

Solly got out his notebook, this should be interesting reading for back home. He watched as men in helmets and men in flat hats came and went, all seemed very intent on where they were going. Those who came out in groups were chatting together, the inevitable constant talk, thought Solly as his pen flew over the pages.

After a while he decided he had enough information about the police station and its men and he got up from the wall, put away his notebook and pen and went over to the town hall. It was a magnificent building, very large, with two great columns on each side of the main doors which were enormous. Solly knew he could not go inside, so instead he watched as again people went in and out of the great doors. Not quite so much to write about here, but he put a little more in his notebook. Tiring of the town hall he decided to move on again.

Going by the side of the police station he wandered along, passing all kinds of people as he did so. Having walked for some distance he stopped to look around, he realised suddenly that it was nearly all men going in his direction, men and boys with a few ladies only. They were wearing red and white scarves and the chatter was loud and shrill.

"We are bound to win, two goals…*at least!* We are the better team, they don't stand a chance!" And so went the comments on all sides as the people passed Solly. He squeezed into a shop doorway and got out his notebook again, well now this was an interesting situation, he quickly wrote in his book.

Then he decided to follow the crowd and fell in behind two large men with red and white scarves on. They hurried along with Solly following them until they stopped at a gate and paid to go into the football ground. Solly did the same, and went after the two men he had followed. They all settled into seats in front of the great green area before them.

The noise was tremendous, not only the endless talk and the shouting, but the singing too combined to give an ear-splitting sound over the whole ground. Then as Solly was about to get out his notebook again, a mighty roar rang out. The teams were on the pitch. Soon the game had started, and as Solly watched not only the teams but the people around him, his pen flew over the pages. He heard one man near him remark to another, 'He must be a reporter,', but Solly just kept writing. A goal was scored and the noise was deafening, the scarves were waved in the air, and the delight of the crowd could be felt.

The game came to half-time, many of the crowd went in search of refreshment, but Solly stayed where he was. Then another whistle blew and the game began again. Soon the opposing team scored to the grumbles of the crowd in red and white scarves.

Solly noted down all the reactions, but before long the team in red and white had given their fans the chance to cheer as they scored once more. This was the final score, and a pleasing one for the home side as Solly could see, as they cheerfully got ready to leave the ground.

His notebook was getting very full now as he put it in his pocket and followed the crowd into the streets.

It was time to go and get something to eat again, and so as they came to the shops Solly began to look for somewhere to go for refreshment. At last he came across a small cosy looking place with red chequered cloths on the tables and decided to go inside. It was quite busy, but after getting himself a sandwich and a drink Solly did find a seat at a table.

Of course he was not alone for long, as he had come to expect, more people came to share his table. This time it was three men who had obviously been to the football match. They sat discussing the merits of the game among themselves, and Solly took out his notebook and pen. He began to write very quickly, and rapidly filled page after page of his book, his ears were open to the conversations around him and his eyes scoured the room again and again observing people as they chatted together, drank their drinks and ate their food.

The three men at his table kept glancing at him, but for once no words were uttered to him, only to each other. Solly finally shut his book and put it away in his pocket with his pen. Getting up from his chair he went outside again, the day was not quite as bright now and people were hurrying in all directions as if they were trying to beat the rain that threatened.

Solly wandered along watching people as he did so, a busker was playing a violin, and people were throwing coins into the case that lay at his feet. This was recorded in Solly's book before he went on to look at a fountain which was throwing water in the air before it fell down into the area around the base. Flower beds were in bloom here in the pedestrian area too.

Solly passed on taking notes of the busy traffic as he came again to the main streets, traffic was snarled up as cars and buses fought for a place in the lanes they needed to go, right, left or straight on.

Big stores were awash with light, and people were still streaming in and out. Going into one of the bigger stores Solly was swept along with the crowd, past racks with every type of clothing, all in colours so varied that it dazzled as it hung in row after row waiting for the shoppers to select and carry off their purchases. There was every item imaginable for sale, and people were buying and walking through the store carrying bags of shopping and chattering to each other.

Of course, the inevitable chatter! thought Solly, always talking together, and always opening their mouths to let sounds come out, never silent. There was no chance of getting out his notebook and pen so he headed for the doors, again being swept along by the tide of people.

Once outside he went and stood in the doorway of a bank, it being closed he was able to do so, no one was trying to rush in or out. Getting out his notebook and pen he made notes on the department store and the people who had been shopping in it.

As he finished he realised that it was perhaps slowing down somewhat, not so many people about now, so Solly decided to catch his bus away from the city and report back.

He headed for the bus stop and joined the queue waiting for the bus. Out came the notebook again, this queueing must be reported too. The bus came and everyone climbed on, some people going upstairs on the double-decker bus, while the less able went inside the lower deck. Solly went upstairs and took a seat, glancing around him he saw a varied selection of passengers, mostly younger people as the older folk had declined to climb the stairs.

Out came the notebook and pen, and Solly made many entries as people went down the stairs when their stops were reached and more people came to take their places.

The bus finally reached its terminus and Solly prepared to leave as did the few remaining passengers still on the bus. It was almost dark now as he went down the road away from the bus stop. Down the road he went, which led to brightly lit houses; how soon

204

it becomes dark and lights are put on here, well, it won't be long before I'm there now, Solly mused as he walked up to the houses.

Near the houses was a hedge with a stile leading to a footpath in the field. Solly climbed over the stile and went across the field to another stile which led into a wood. Going through the wood he pondered on his day and all the notes he had taken, he hoped they would be satisfactory and help to show how people lived and how they behaved.

Beyond the wood was a field again, it was a small field with scrub growing everywhere, broom abounded here and nothing else could have grown, nor yet was it suitable for grazing ground. A black shape was in the centre of the field, Solly strode towards it. As he approached light appeared and a humming noise could be heard.

Standing in front of the shape, Solly waited, then held up both arms, a door slid open and he walked inside the big black space ship.

How glad he would be to get rid of this silly human form, what a stupid shape humans were. *And all that talking!* All they had to do on his own planet was to look at someone and thoughts were transferred. If they did not want thoughts read, then they were not, all the constant opening and closing of people's mouths here was quite disconcerting.

Having to adopt human form so he could mingle with them

had not been easy, but his own race was far superior to these Earth beings who walked upright.

Well, here he was, back again, and now for his report. But first to become himself again.

Solly went into a chamber and felt the vibrations moving around him, soon he was himself again, a true Tryonad. How glad he would be to return to his own planet.

He crept out of the chamber on all fours and went forward to give his report.

The End

Lucky Seven

The seventh child of a seventh child is told that she should have special powers, but is that a gift or a curse?

Sarah felt very disgruntled. Why did they all keep going on and on about this? What did they expect her to do? She was sick of hearing about it!

Her mother had told her first of all, "Do you know you are the seventh child of a seventh child, Sarah? You are supposed to possess some special power. Usually it is being able to heal people who are ill, or if not that, then you can tell fortunes or look into the future and tell us what is going to happen. But you certainly will have something special about you."

Sarah remembered her childhood, the teacups thrust into her hands by relatives and neighbours all expecting a reading, the disappointment when all she saw was tea leaves.

Then Aunty Paula dragging her upstairs in the terraced house where she lived, to see Uncle Mike who was suffering from some medical condition they all sadly shook their heads about.

"Put your hands on his chest, Sarah, you should be able to heal you know… the seventh of a seventh…" so said Aunty Paula. She had screwed her eyes tightly shut and said under her breath 'get better, get better' but nothing happened to make her uncle better. Uncle Mike had died a month later and Sarah had felt the reproachful looks of all her relatives at the funeral.

Even then they hadn't left her alone about it. Every time inflation went up they asked her when it would improve. When one country fell out with another they asked her what the outcome would be. And so it went on, by the time Sarah was in her teens she was heartily sick of it all. When will they realise I have no special power? she asked herself.

Then she met Patrick, he was wonderful, and when she told him about her problem he howled with laughter. "Never mind, Sarah, you will always be special to me," he said.

After a happy courtship they settled down to married life, and except for an occasional reminder from her mother or aunty, Sarah was allowed to forget she was the seventh child of a seventh child.

Her first daughter, Coral, brought joy to them both, but by the time her second daughter Louise was born the magic was going out of her marriage. Patrick was irritated that the home wasn't always tidy, he moaned both about the baby crying and little Louise toddling around and getting under his feet. In fact he was always moaning, thought Sarah.

For the first time in ages she thought of the special powers she was supposed to possess, and concentrated really hard one day, directing her thoughts to Patrick and wishing him to be the same man she had married. But her 'special powers' were not working any better than before and Patrick did not change at all.

Then he started bringing Simon home with him. Simon was single and he worked with Patrick at the insurance office in town.

From the very first meeting Sarah didn't like him. The way he brushed the chair with his hand before sitting down, the firm way he put little Louise away from him when she toddled over to see him, and the disdainful way he looked around their home was quite enough to show Sarah he was not a nice man, yet he and Patrick got along so well.

Patrick's complaints got worse and were now interspersed with "Simon says if you put Louise down for a nap in the afternoon she wouldn't be so bad tempered," or "Simon says if you got up a little earlier you could get a good start on the housework before the children woke up," and on and on until she wanted to scream.

She began to dread Simon coming over. He lived in a beautiful bachelor flat, so Patrick said, and she detested the envy in Patrick's voice.

No matter that she made extra effort to cook her husband's favourite meals and tried to make herself look attractive, Patrick seemed obsessed with Simon's way of life.

One day after an argument with Patrick, who again had quoted Simon, she sat at the kitchen table seething. Both little girls were having a nap (not due to Simon's advice either, she thought angrily) when suddenly the thoughts of her supposed special powers entered her head. But what use are they anyway? she asked herself, they couldn't help me overcome this problem even if I was capable of something extraordinary. Eventually she shook herself out of her deep thoughts and carried on with her usual routine.

Patrick was no better when he came home, and Sarah was surprised to find herself thinking how peaceful it was when he was at work. Lately he was a nuisance at home, she had tried, oh how she'd tried to make things right. But he seemed to be always whining. He sounded like the silly game they had played as children. "Simon says, Simon says..." Wouldn't it be great if she and *her* daughters, for she had come to think of them as such, could be without this man who never seemed to notice her and the children anymore, except to complain?

Then she felt ashamed, for Patrick hadn't really been too bad before Simon came to work with him. She felt sure he would have stopped complaining if Simon had not been there, and she loved Patrick.

Her mother came the next day to tell her that Aunty Paula was ill and to ask, "Can you do anything, Sarah? All she says is that she wants to join Uncle Mike."

To please her mother, Sarah said she would visit Aunt Paula on the following day. When she arrived with her daughters, Aunt Paula was in bed and she looked very ill. Sarah sat next to her and held her hand, but her aunt seemed no better for all the effort of Sarah's wishful thoughts.

Her mother phoned the next day to say her aunty had died. She was sorry about Aunty Paula, and that night as she laid in bed beside Patrick her mind in turmoil, she wished, oh how she wished she was able to make changes. As she drifted off to sleep she thought of Simon and his negative influence on Patrick.

The following day, Patrick phoned from his office at lunchtime, he was shocked and very upset. He told her that Simon had not come in to the office, and being worried at hearing nothing from him, he and a colleague had gone round to his flat. Getting no answer to their knocking, they had broken in to find Simon dead, apparently having died the evening before.

When Patrick arrived home he was shaken but he took Sarah in his arms saying, "These two deaths so close together made me realise how lucky we are. I have you and two lovely daughters. I am glad to be alive. Sorry I've been grumpy lately, I have been supporting Simon who was ill, but I have you and Coral and Louise and I am lucky. I love you all."

Sarah couldn't believe it, yes she was sorry about Simon, but at least Patrick had come back to her.

That night when the girls had been put to bed by both Patrick and herself, and they sat as they had not done for a long time, close together on the couch, something kept niggling at the back of her mind.

Patrick had told her that Simon had left a letter saying he hoped to die before the terminal illness he had made him a complete invalid, he had been told that it could be a year, or perhaps less, and that he would suffer greatly if it was longer rather than shorter. But he had not taken his own life, he had died in his sleep. The letter was in Simon's wallet, addressed to Patrick, and also thanked him for his friendship.

It all became clear at last to Sarah as her mind went back over the years, Uncle Mike's whispered message as she put her hands on his chest. "Let me die in peace, lass." Then her aunts words when she had visited her. "Let me join Mike now." She remembered her father after his dreadful stroke saying, "I can't move much, lass, and I know I never will. It's time for me to go." And Simon on his last visit had said, "I would like to die while I can still be me." She assumed it to be a mere philosophical discussion, but she had put her hand on his shoulder as she passed the chair where he sat, just as she had put hands on the others who had wished to die.

Now she knew what her 'gift' was. A seventh child of a seventh child indeed she was. But was it a gift or a curse?

The End

Temperate Feeling

A young woman visits a botanic garden built on the site of a former hospital and experiences some very unusual sensations and an otherworldly message.

There was a strange feeling here, a feeling of sadness. As Christine walked along by the flower beds the sadness became more intense.

She knew that there had once been a hospital here, complete with its own chapel. People had been sent here to be treated and to hopefully recover from the 'chest disease' as it was then known. Tuberculosis. Now the disease had all but been eliminated, and there was no need for a hospital anymore that specialized in only one area of medicine.

So the blocks of buildings had been pulled down, the land levelled and left until the council decided to use this area for gardens, a museum, gift shop and tea rooms. They also built a huge 'Temperate House' for special plants, right on the spot where the operating theatre had once stood.

All this Christine knew from the local people she had talked to, and from books she had read about the area, so now she was having a look for herself.

Having wandered around by the central pond, along the paths between the flower beds, past huge trees magnificent in their rich summer leaves, (they must have been here for years, she thought) her steps had taken her to the huge Temperate House towering above the flower beds.

Slowly she walked along the side of it, and suddenly felt as

216

if she was going to burst into tears. Whatever is wrong with me? she thought, it's a lovely day, I have nothing to cry for. But the tears were rolling down her cheeks. Christine walked over to a garden bench and sat down; gradually she felt better and decided to go home to her small flat in the nearby town where she lived.

Her mother had died from cancer when she was still at school, her father had remarried and moved away when she was eighteen, after first making sure she was settled in her own place. There were weekly phone calls to her father and occasional visits for holidays. Christmas and birthday cards being the only contact with her Aunt Sue, her mother's sister, who lived in Scotland over a hundred miles away.

But she wasn't lonely, she enjoyed her work at the bank and belonged to swimming, tennis and poetry clubs.

The thought of the strange feeling in the gardens kept coming into Christine's mind, even at work where she was reprimanded for her lack of concentration. So the first time she was free, she went back to the gardens and headed for the area that had affected her so much. Sure enough, as soon as she started along the same path, the feeling of overwhelming sadness returned. Christine tried to fight against it. I'm here, alive and well, the sun is shining, *I'm happy* she told herself.

But the tears pouring down her cheeks were of a great sadness, a helpless feeling swamped her as she walked along by the huge Temperate House. A lady coming towards her stopped as she drew close. "Are you alright, dear? Don't you feel well?"

Christine nodded her head and fled back to the car park where she sat in her small car composing herself before she felt able to drive home.

She made some more enquiries about the garden and about the hospital that had once stood there. Some of the older towns people were pleased to talk to her about it, and told her stories of the lovely old buildings with their tall chimneys, the patients who had walked in the grounds, the open days for visitors, and what a shame they thought it was to have pulled it all down.

There were others who would rather not speak of it at all, and one particular older man who said she would be better not knowing. But after some coaxing he told her stories of how some of the patients had horrible things done to them as part of their experimental treatment, and that when the operating theatre had been pulled down, there had been strange sightings and loud moaning sounds, which were so frightening that some workmen refused to work there at all.

As he began to expand on his tale, Christine could not tell the difference between what he really knew, and what he had added to embroider the story for her benefit.

She realised that a lot of people must have suffered while at the hospital, and some must have died, but she did not believe in ghosts or the supernatural. She had told no one how she felt when in the gardens for fear of being laughed at, but she did persuade a friend to go with her one evening after work, just for a walk.

They arrived in the car park and ambled slowly around the gardens admiring the various displays of flowers. Sheila was a keen gardener, so was full of chatter about what she would put in her own garden if she could. Without saying anything, Christine guided her friend along the paths until they came to the one leading to the Temperate House.

Again Christine felt the terrible sadness and the desperate longing to cry, but Sheila was still chatting away quite happily, and other people passed by with no sign of anything being wrong at all. The feeling was getting stronger and Christine knew she had to get away before she made a fool of herself. So taking Sheila's arm she said, "How about a cup of tea? They serve a really good afternoon tea here." And she led her friend away.

"Are you alright, Chris?" Sheila asked. "You look a little upset."

"Yes, I'm fine, it's the herb garden, something in it always affects my eyes. Now, how about a scone or a biscuit with your tea?"

After taking Sheila home, Christine went home too, but could not stop thinking of the garden. The next day she went back again.

As she walked down the path to the Temperate House, there were once again tears and this time a heavy feeling in her chest, as if someone was pressing on it, feeling panicked she left.

But as the months went by and summer turned to autumn, she found herself returning again and again. It was always the same. The sadness, the tears, the crushing feeling in her chest, and now she was starting to think that she felt someone nearby when she stood in a particular spot.

This is ridiculous, she thought, it's becoming an obsession with me. Even if I believed in the afterlife, which I don't, surely by now I would know something more. She went to the local library to find out anything she could about the gardens. There were some books about the old hospital, and lots of information, but nothing shed any light on her personal experiences. She tried reading books on theories of the afterlife, ghosts and spirits, but nothing gave her the answer she was seeking.

On a warm Sunday afternoon she set out for the gardens alone, determined she would stay in the area that made her so sad and see what happened instead of moving away when the feeling overwhelmed her.

It was quite busy in the gardens, people were walking and talking, no one seemed unduly bothered about being near the Temperate House, just a general enjoyment of an autumn afternoon.

She went to have tea first, and sat in the open air just watching people come and go. There were families, elderly couples, some foreign visitors, a mixed crowd really, but everyone seemed well and fairly happy. People began to drift away as the afternoon passed into early evening, and after a slow walk around the gardens looking at the late season's show of flowers, Christine went down the path that had become so familiar to her. No one was around now, and there was a definite chill in the air, but having come prepared she put on her coat.

She sat down on a bench near the area that was, to her, so strangely emotional, and closed her eyes trying to picture what it must have been like when the hospital was here. She shivered, opening her eyes; it was almost dusk, that peculiar time when it is still light but not daylight anymore. The Temperate House looked like a monstrosity in this light. Christine walked towards it and stood near the doors. It was locked for the night, no one else was around and she knew that as her car was in the car park someone would be looking to see who was still in the gardens.

Then the feeling came again, the awful sadness, the tears, and the heavy weight on her chest. She stood her ground, suddenly she saw coming around the side of the Temperate House a nurse wearing a white apron and cap, her arms outstretched to Christine. She was young, pretty and smiling. As she came closer she held her hands out, instinctively Christine held hers out too, she felt the coldness as her hands were covered by the ones reaching for hers, then a soft cool breeze passing over, and it seemed, *through her*. Slowly she turned around to see the nurse walking away, but she was not alone.

By her side was another young woman who looked over her shoulder at Christine, that look was one she would never forget. Thank you. Happiness. Relief. All seemed to be in that one fleeting glance. Then they were gone, no sounds of footsteps fading away, just silence.

Christine felt a sense of calm come over her, she knew what she needed to do. Somehow there would be no more tears for her here, the message had been passed, received, and through her, would be acted upon. The patients and their gentle nurses had to be acknowledged. She would ensure a memorial was placed right here in the garden to honour them. A fountain surrounded by flowers, yes that was it. And a statue, a lovely young nurse reaching kindly out to her patients. They would not be forgotten.

A voice made her jump. "Hey there, time to go, miss. Is that your car in the car park?" It was a gardener. Christine apologized and turned to go home, now she knew why she had felt compelled to keep going back to the gardens, and as the sun descended behind the horizon, all was at peace.

The End

Spring Clean

A husband's frustration with his constantly cleaning wife is quickly abated with a view of the other side of the coin.

Spring was here at last, the signs were everywhere. The snowdrops had gone, the daffodils had bloomed and faded, and now the trees had new leaves; the fresh almost pale yellow of the oak, the darker green of the elder, and there was an overall feeling that winter had been banished.

There was only one thing wrong with that, thought Jack as he cycled home from work admiring nature's wonders as he rode along. Eileen would be at it again. Spring cleaning she called it, turning everything upside down was what *he* called it.

Sure enough when he reached home and went into the kitchen, no delightful aroma of dinner cooking reached him, only the chemical smell of cleaning. Down on her knees was Eileen, washing out a cupboard, and every surface in the kitchen was covered with plates, dishes and crockery of every kind.

"I didn't know we had so much stuff," he said. "You're at it again, as soon as spring starts arriving everywhere has to be cleaned!"

"Now then, Jack, do you want to live in a dirty house? Do you want to get things out for our visitors and find that everything is dusty?"

"Fat chance of that, Eileen, nothing gets the time to gather dust here, in fact if I stay still too long, I'm sure you would dust or wash me and put me away."

"Oh, Jack, I'm sorry, I didn't even see how late it was. You go and wash your hands and I'll put these away and get us something to eat."

Not the meal he'd expected, but after eating a quickly prepared dinner, Jack felt better and suggested a walk to his wife. They set off along the lane, watching the spring lambs playing in the fields and seeing the birds flying about in a hurry carrying twigs to build their nests. Spring was so busy for them all.

As they slowly walked on, climbing over a stile and crossing a field, they realised someone was in front of them. It was old Mr. James who lived in the village, alone now as his wife had died a few years ago. He was walking with Tess his spaniel. They caught up with him and were shocked to see how neglected he looked, his coat had a button missing, one shoe had half a lace, and he had not shaved that day. After a few words they parted company and Mr. James headed back where they had come from.

The next day as Jack cycled along the lane home from work, he again felt how wonderful spring was in all its newness.

But once he was home, Eileen was again involved in cleaning, it was the food cupboard this time. However, dinner was simmering on the stove. Jack sighed, he might as well grin and bear it, for nothing would stop Eileen when she got the spring cleaning bug.

After dinner, again they went for a walk and were surprised

to see Mr. James's dog, Tess, out on her own in the field. Calling her to them they decided to take her back to where she lived.

The cottage where Mr. James lived was even more remote than their own, and when they got there it was to see the door wide open. Hurrying inside they saw Mr. James lying on the floor, he was groaning and in obvious pain. Jack tried to make him more comfortable without moving him too much while Eileen phoned for the ambulance. He had fallen and broken his hip when he came home and could not move, he had been there for some time, he said. Soon he was whisked away to hospital, Jack and Eileen promised to take care of his dog and lock up his house for him.

When he had gone Jack looked around the cottage, poor old chap, his home was in a bad way. The dust was thick and the curtains needed washing, but it wasn't for him to say anything about it. There was no one to help Mr. James though, as he had no relatives, so he vowed that he and Eileen must keep an eye on him in future.

They took Tess home with them after locking up, and agreed they would go to see Mr. James on the morrow.

Jack took another look around his own home before going to bed, and had another think about Eileen's spring cleaning, all was bright and clean. After all, if nature had a new start in spring—wasn't that a kind of spring clean? After the trees had shed all their leaves and let everything lie still for the winter, spring was surely

Mother Earth starting afresh, wouldn't it be wrong not to follow her example and make your home bright and clean too?

He would look with new eyes at Eileen and her cleaning every spring from now on, after seeing what happened when no one did it. Yes, he would also keep an eye on the old chap, and see if perhaps he and Eileen together could spring clean for him too. There were lots of ways of being useful, and keeping an eye on the old fellow in future would be one of them.

Spring—he loved it, thought Jack. And the cleaning? Well, nature does it, so why not?

The End

Kidnapped

A small boy in Victorian England faces hardship and hunger
before finding happiness.

The boy sat on the cold stone wall, leaves scurrying around his feet. It was autumn and he was cold and hungry.

Thoughts of the thatched cottage he had left crept into Ben's mind, and of his Aunt Bess, cousins Rufus, Meg, Beth and Josef. Ben had gone to live there when he was three, now he was eight, and times had changed. His aunt had told him about his mother and father who had sent him to stay with her when they had caught the 'chest disease' and began coughing up blood. "It will only be for a while," his mother had said in the note she had sent her sister, "To make sure Ben is safe from the disease." But they didn't get better, he was an orphan and he had remained with his aunt.

Aunt Bess had told him about his mother, how pretty she was, and how a gentleman who been visiting the local vicar (who she had worked for as a housemaid) had met and fallen for her, married her, and taken her to live in the town where Ben was born. No words were spoken of others from his father's family. Aunt Bess said they didn't like him marrying a country girl.

Uncle Will had not minded Ben staying, he was off fishing every day and saw little of his family, but he was a pleasant man. The only one who didn't like Ben was cousin Rufus; he resented him being part of the family.

Then the day came when it all changed, a storm sprang up

230

while Uncle Will was fishing, he and his crew drowned and his boat was lost. Aunt Bess was distraught, she had loved Will, they'd had a good life with their family but now in her grief she shut herself off, unable to cope.

The running of the house fell on cousin Meg, the support of the family on Rufus who was fifteen. He had worked on a farm from age thirteen, having no love of the sea, but without his father's income it had become a struggle to feed six mouths.

One day he came into the house and told Ben to fetch water from the well, he was always ordering everyone about and saying he was the man of the house now. With a struggle, Ben fetched the water, but as he came through the door he tripped over Rufus who had his legs outstretched. Water went everywhere and Rufus went mad, he hit Ben over and over again wherever he could reach him as Ben crouched on the floor in terror. Then he kicked him. No one dared to stop him, and when he picked Ben up from the floor shouting, "Why should I feed you?" and flung him out, everyone just cringed or burst into tears.

Now here he was, bruised and hungry with nowhere to go, and night was drawing in. Painfully he stood up, and then walked on down the lane he had come along. On and on he walked, soon it was dark and he needed shelter for the night. He saw a light ahead and stumbled across a field towards it. Suddenly there was a skittering sound as an animal moved in front of him, it was a sheep and he was near a farm.

231

At last he reached the farm yard, hoping to find the barn for a night's rest and maybe a raw turnip or potato to eat. He found the barn and went inside, at least he was out of the wind. There was a trough with clean water and a pile of potatoes in a corner, quickly washing some of them he ate hungrily, then climbed to the back of the barn on a pile of soft hay. Sleep came quickly, but not for long. The barn door was flung violently open and a man stood there with a lamp. Ben shrank away but he had been seen.

"I knew someone was here, my dog was sniffing at the door and whining. Come here. Who are you?" he demanded. Ben came forward and told his story, he was roughly grabbed by the shoulder of his tattered jacket. "Right, you can work for me then." He was taken to the house and locked in an attic room.

The next few months were a nightmare for Ben, he fed the animals, cleaned out the pigsties and cow byre, ran around doing what he was bid until he dropped with exhaustion each night. The dog was always near him, if he tried to move away from the farm it snarled and then barked until Jed the owner who lived alone came to see what was happening.

Ben was growing up fast and the hard work was making him fit, for Jed at least fed him well. One day after a hard time working in the frost, Ben knew he had to do something. It was February and snow was in the air, but he was determined to leave now and get away from this hard life.

When he had again been locked in his attic room for the night with the dog on guard outside his door, he put his plan to work. The windows were fastened tight, but with the sharp prong from a pitchfork he had broken, he had been working on the window frame for weeks now and he was nearly through. The old wood finally gave way and quietly he opened the window. Carefully he scrambled down the trailing creeper vines and was gone. Not stopping all night he put a lot of distance between himself, Jed, and the dog.

The next day he was sleeping in a ditch when a gruff voice and a hand shaking him woke him up. Opening his eyes he saw an old vagabond. "Who are you, lad? Where are you going?" This time Ben was more cautious, only saying he was a homeless orphan. "Come along, lad, I'll take care of you." The man gave him a piece of bread to eat.

For a while Ben didn't mind the old vagabond's company, they travelled on together, stopping in villages and towns begging for food. Often Ben would run around offering to fetch and carry for anyone who would give him food in exchange. Sometimes he carried parcels, sometimes he drove sheep into a field, anything to keep alive. But he realised he was keeping the two of them, and it was harder than keeping one. He began to understand what Rufus had felt, but not the way he had acted.

So one day he told Abel he was going away, and left the old vagabond with enough food for the day so he wouldn't be hungry.

He had been given some old clothes in payment for work he had done and was managing to keep warm, winter would soon be gone now, it was warmer already and he was quite tough after sleeping out in barns for so long.

The next town he came to was busy, he wandered along looking for any chance to earn bread and somewhere he could stay for a while. Feeling tired, Ben sat on a doorstep until a voice nearby made him jump.

"What are you doing?" a well-dressed boy was asking.

Ben got up. "Just sitting."

"Well, that's my house. Where do you live?"

"Nowhere," said Ben and began to move away.

"Stay and talk for a while, I'm lonely. My name is Barnaby and I don't have any family, only my father."

Ben sat down again, the boys began to chat and Ben told his new friend about himself. Barnaby took Ben inside his home, it was very nice, better than the thatched cottage of Aunt Bess even. Before he knew it, Ben was washed and dressed in some of Barnaby's clothes and eating a hearty meal.

"I've never seen anyone eat as much as that!" Barnaby laughed. The housekeeper stood by with a grim face waiting for Mr. Flounders to come home, orders were orders, and she had obeyed the young master of the house, but that would change when his father came home.

Mr. Flounders was astonished to find his son's new friend, but agreed to let him stay the night and no more. So, in spite of Barnaby's pleading, Ben left the next day.

Ben decided to stay around town for a while and on his wanderings came across a Punch and Judy showman setting up for his act. The man was grumbling to himself under his breath. "No help, how can I do it all? My missus laid up sick but I have to earn a crust."

Ben went up to the man. "Can I help? I've nothing else to do. If you will only give me something to eat for helping?"

After shaking his head then turning his back, the man found he could not get his screen up. "Boy! Help me today and then we'll see," he said turning back to Ben.

The next few weeks were good for Ben. He enjoyed helping with the show, collecting coins from the crowd who gathered each time, and the good food, shelter and kindness of Mr. and Mrs. Shuttleworth. But as the good lady became stronger the couple talked of moving on again, there was no permanent place for Ben. The day came and off they went. Ben was alone again, but at least it was summer now.

For a while Ben tried offering to carry again, or to do any jobs available, but it was getting harder to find any work. He wandered down to the smithy and offered to help in return for his food, but he wasn't needed. Day after day he went, watching the farrier shoeing the horses, only leaving long enough to find food.

Sam the farrier came over to him after a week of this. "Alright! As you are so keen and not afraid of hard work, you can pump the bellows." Ben was delighted and he worked hard. Sam let him sleep in the forge, and he loved it. Week after week he worked and then it was winter again. How glad he was of the warm shelter of the forge.

Spring came at last after a very hard winter. Ben knew he would not have survived out in the open, and thought about his vagabond friend, hoping he was alright.

One day he was leading a horse back to the inn after it had been shod, when a voice called, "Ben, Ben!" He saw Barnaby waving to him and went to talk to his young friend. "Where have you been, Ben? I've been looking for you and so has my father, he has someone he wants you to meet." Ben explained he had to deliver the horse and then get back to the forge, but would go to see Barnaby and his father that night.

When he finally did get to Mr. Flounders' home he was very tired, but knocked on the door and waited. Barnaby himself answered, and was so excited that Ben wondered what was amiss.

Going into the house there was a grey-haired man standing with Barnaby's father. "How are you, Ben?" he asked. Then he began his explanation. This was Ben's grandfather. His anger at his son marrying a village girl had soon dissipated when he lost Ben's father to the chest disease. He was so very sorry and had tried to find Ben, but no one seemed to know where he was. Then when he had finally traced him to Aunt Bess, it was to find that he had gone again. No one said where or why, and Ben's grandfather thought he must have been kidnapped.

When Barnaby's father had told him of the boy who had come in with his son, and related his story, he was sure it was his grandson. But Ben had already moved on.

Would Ben like to go and live with his grandparents? he wanted to know. And yes, he had a grandmother as well who was desperate to meet him! He would live around the corner from Barnaby. His grandfather understood and admired his attitude when he said he had to go on the morrow to explain to the farrier. But from tonight onwards he had a family, a warm bed, new clothes, plenty to eat and whole new future ahead of him.

The End

Autumn Years

A couple in their autumn years discover that worrying about the future is unnecessary.

The countryside was at its best now, all the autumn colours were everywhere, gold and russet, through to brown. Strolling across the fields together Hannah felt they were very much in tune with their surroundings. Graham was sixty-four and she was two years younger, really in the autumn of their years.

I wonder if the leaves feel as they fall to the ground that although they are no longer fresh and green, they are still the same, even when they are discoloured by age? She laughed aloud at her silly thoughts and Graham looked over at her, smiling as he did so.

No explanations were asked for or given, they knew each other so well after forty years of marriage, or did they? For a moment a frown replaced the laughter.

She loved it so much here in the village where they had lived for twenty-five years, but now Graham was talking of moving to the large town ten miles away near their only child, Graham junior, who was married and settled comfortably in a house on the outskirts of town where he worked as a solicitor.

What did age matter really when you were happy where you lived, why change? Was it that Graham had not been happy living here all these years? She cast her mind back, he had never complained about commuting, and having retired early two years ago seemed delighted they could spend time together walking in the woods and fields around their home.

240

They stopped at the fast running stream, how clear it was, she knew that it was here that badger, fox and all the local wildlife came to drink.

Graham squeezed her hand, "Time to go back, it gets dark so early now." Slowly they began to walk home. Climbing over the stile back into the lane they saw a movement ahead of them.

It was a close neighbour of theirs, Mrs. Bettison and she was limping, they hurried forward to offer help. Her black Labrador Sark came anxiously to meet them wagging his tail; he was Mrs. Bettison's only companion since her husband had died not long ago.

Mrs. Bettison smiled at them. "I'm afraid I have hurt my ankle, we were enjoying our walk when I lost my balance."

Graham hurried to give his support and they slowly made their way back to Mrs. Bettison's house. She was soon settled in an armchair in her home, her ankle bathed and bandaged and a cup of hot tea in her hand.

"Well, you haven't broken anything so a good rest should soon put it right, but just to be sure we will have the doctor call in tomorrow," said Graham.

After making sure she had everything she needed they went home, promising to call in the next day. Hannah was very quiet while getting their evening meal and as they sat down at the table Graham asked if she was alright.

"I see why you are worried now, Graham. Poor Mrs. Bettison has no one, and just a small accident means you are very vulnerable. Is that why you wanted us to move so that if either of us are left alone we have someone to help?"

Graham sighed, "The thought had crossed my mind, one of us will surely be left alone someday, what then, Hannah?" The rest of the evening had an air of disquiet about it for both of them.

The next morning they quickly did the chores so they could go to see their neighbour. What a surprise when they arrived, there were so many people there. The postman had called to deliver a small package from Mrs. Bettison's sister in Canada. When she had hobbled over to answer the door he had discovered her accident, and no telegram could have worked faster to spread the news as he rapidly delivered both the mail and the news throughout the village.

The offers of help were many, and if Sark had been taken on all the walks offered he would have finished up at Land's End or John O'Groats. Soon it was all settled and Mrs. Bettison had a rotating schedule of people to help her.

Coming away, Graham and Hannah began to realise how many friends they too had. They caught their bus into the next town where they met their daughter-in-law as promised for lunch at a restaurant.

Ann was very nice, they got on very well and discussed

242

many topics before it became obvious she wanted to say something but wasn't sure how to begin.

Graham mentioned his son's work and Ann seized her chance. "I have something to tell you both, Graham junior feels we should wait, but it only gets harder to say if you put things off."

She went on to say there was no chance of children for them at all as tests had proved she could not have any, and they had decided to make a new life without a family. They were moving to a city practice where the younger Graham had better prospects than in the small town where they lived at present. Ann had also applied for and been offered a better job so they would soon be moving further away and they both hoped that Hannah and Graham would understand. What else could they say but yes, of course they did?

Both Graham and Hannah were quiet on the journey home. After their evening meal young Graham rang them, they were on the telephone for a long time. After Graham replaced the receiver they sat looking at each other.

"Well, Graham, it seems we have two choices, move to the city or stay here," said Hannah. They agreed to give each other time to think and went to bed.

The next day they went to see Mrs. Bettison and take Sark for a walk as promised. She was looking much better and told them the doctor had diagnosed a sprain and everyone was being wonderful.

They went for a walk with Sark who was quite happy to go with them. It was a cold crisp day, the leaves were crackling underfoot and nature's colours were standing out sharp and clear.

"Graham, would you rather have busy streets, lots of traffic, crowded shops, occasional visits with young Graham and Ann when they can spare the time from their busy new lives, or would you rather have your twilight years here among the beauty of nature and our friends?"

Graham looked at her, and thought how worried young Graham had sounded on the telephone last night, children had to have their own lives and he and Hannah already had theirs, right here.

"We're happy here, aren't we?" he asked.

Hannah nodded.

"Then who needs more than that?"

"You're right, our autumn years should be spent exactly where we want to be."

That evening they rang young Graham, they knew they had done the right thing by the relief in his voice. He wanted them to be happy, he knew they were settled where they lived and spoke of how he and Ann would enjoy coming to stay for long weekends and holidays.

Ann came on the telephone to ask if they were quite sure about it, and to say she hoped to see them for lunch the following week in town again.

Putting the telephone down, they smiled at each other.

"Well, Graham, how about getting ourselves organised now. We have a busy schedule which includes taking Sark on our walks and seeing his owner each day. There are new evening classes at the village hall and the local drama group is looking for volunteers to help with the new play."

They both began to laugh and relax, nothing needed to change after all, and all was well in their world.

The End

The Last Waltz

A tired lady enjoys a quiet day in the park and a last waltz with a gentle stranger.

Amy sat down on the bench, what a lovely park this was, and fancy finding it here. The walk she had set out on today had taken her much further than she had intended to go.

A bird was singing in the tree by her side, Amy tried to put a name with the sound. Ah, yes, it was a song thrush, dear, dear, she was getting quite forgetful! When she had been younger it would have been no trouble to identify the bird and its song. She leaned back and closed her eyes, how peaceful it was here with no one else about and the lovely warm sunshine, it would be so easy to fall asleep.

There surely had not been a park here when she was young? She struggled to remember, no, there had been just open fields. The town had been small then, her cousin who lived with her now had left for the city saying it was boring living in a small town. But they had built more and more onto the town in recent years. She did not like to come in this direction normally, no wonder she had missed this park. Away at the far end was a children's playground, but here it was just lush grass, flower beds and trees.

Suddenly, aware of someone sitting down beside her she opened her eyes. A grey-haired man was there on the seat, he smiled as she glanced at him and she nodded a greeting.

They both sat silently, watching the butterflies flit about

248

and listening to the lovely bird's song. Did it never get tired of singing?

Then the man spoke, "Lovely day, isn't it?"

Amy replied, "Yes indeed, a pleasure to be out." She thought to herself how typically British, always polite remarks about the weather, but I hope he doesn't want to start a conversation, I was enjoying the quiet until he came along.

But he did start a conversation, and went on to say, "What a pretty park this is, don't you think so? It's a pleasure to come here, isn't it?"

She sighed inwardly, was there no getting away from people anywhere? Why couldn't they leave you alone sometimes? Yes, there were people who were desperately lonely, she had read about them in the national papers, they needed friends, someone to talk to, but everyone wasn't like that.

My word, after living year after year with her parents, then her mother's sister who came to stay permanently, followed by cousin Ruby who came back after her saying she was 'sick of city life' because she couldn't stand living on her own, Amy needed some peace from it all.

Funny how she'd often been told, 'You're the best at organising the house', and a thousand and one other jobs, or so it seemed. The compliments had long since ceased but she was still the cook, cleaner, housemaid, and in fact, she spent all her time looking after the four adults at home. So it was nice to get away for a walk and some peace whenever she could, a break away from home was a must.

So here she was, hoping for a quiet hour by herself, but now it was broken by this man. Should she get up and walk away? But she felt so tired, perhaps if she just smiled an answer he would go on his way instead. She smiled at the smartly dressed man who smiled gently back at her.

But he was not to be put off. "Have you seen the trees over there with the blossoms on them? Aren't they a pretty sight?" She looked to where he was pointing, yes, the trees were beautiful, shimmering in the slight breeze and heavy with blossoms.

"Well, it is May, isn't it? And this is the month for blossoms," she said.

Amy felt really weary and wished she had not walked as far as she had; she closed her eyes again hoping he would take the hint. All was quiet and she felt the peace that comes before sleep, she began to drift but a hand on her arm made her open her eyes.

"Don't get cold now, will you? It's still early in the season to be sitting outside for long."

Amy straightened up on the seat, she felt stiff, perhaps it was colder than she had realised, she really ought to be getting back. The man had risen but was still looking down at her.

"Don't worry," she said. "I must be going home soon
250

anyway, I have stayed too long. My family will be wondering where I am." Or more likely why I am not there to get tea ready, she thought.

The man sat down again, "Do you have children? Are you married? You have no wedding ring on."

Somehow she found herself telling him how she had wanted to marry, but her parents' demands had given her no chance to meet anyone when she was young. Now in her middle years she felt it was too late, and with four people at home to care for as well, that's why she was so tired.

Her new friend leaned over and patted her hand. "Life seems so unfair, and always to the wrong people. Those who deserve the best get the worst, and those who deserve the worst get the best. Or so it seems," he said.

They sat quietly side by side, the bird had gone from the tree beside them but the trees with their blossoms still shimmered.

Amy closed her eyes again and let the feeling of peace steal over her, it was good to be here in the fresh air. Suddenly there was a full chorus of bird song, she reluctantly came back from the edge of sleep and opened her eyes.

"The evening chorus, I presume?" she said.

It was indeed a chorus, a joyful burst, lovely to hear, and Amy suddenly felt better for her rest, the lovely day, and her new friend who still sat beside her.

She stood up. "It almost makes you feel like dancing, I used to like dancing when I was a teenager."

He stood then and bowed to her. "May I have the pleasure, madam?"

With a giggle Amy stepped forward, no one else was about; everyone must have gone home for tea. So why not? This day was special, she felt.

They waltzed down the path toward the row of trees heavy with blossoms, still shimmering and showering petals on the path. Good thing my parents can't see me now, she thought, then the thought vanished as her feet left the ground and her tiredness was gone, and she was looking down on the trees from above. A beautiful light surrounded her and her new friend was saying, "Welcome, Amy. I was sent to meet you and help you cross over, no more tiredness, no more worry, just peace."

The park keeper doing his rounds before locking the gates was startled to find the lady asleep on the bench. Usually it was down and outs who tried to stay in the park. He soon realised she was not sleeping, and the blue lips told their story. But he could not understand the look on her face.

No sign of suffering, no weary look, just an expression of pure joy, that's what he told his wife later. It was just happiness, and it seemed right somehow because the birds were still singing and some of the blossoms from the trees had settled on her lap.

252

"Really peaceful it all seemed, though it made me late home sorting the ambulance for her. But wherever she's gone, she was pleased to be there and maybe we shouldn't worry about when we die, from the way she looked there is no need. No need at all."

The End

Comes 'The End'

Visitors from another planet infiltrate Earth, but soon discover that they are not the most powerful beings in the universe after all.

The sun was shining brightly, it was an August morning with clear skies and a promise of summer continuing. Nothing seemed any different, people strolling along, children laughing, the penitent on their way to church.

How strange that everyone followed the patterns they were taught as children, learn to talk, walk, feed and dress yourself, go to school, work, live, die. Yes, humans were no better than the lower animals that followed each other across a field, all doing the same thing. Yet how superior they thought they were with their superficial existence and power over lesser animals.

How pitiful their little brains, their reasoning and their need to dominate always. How many wars had there been, still were, ever would be? To fight against their own kind all the time was something they always seemed to want to do. Pity they had not cleared the planet by their actions, but they hadn't. So we must.

He walked along the street looking like any other middle-aged man on a Sunday morning, yet the human eyes were not operational, the nose did not work either, only the mouth was working, fitted with its special box to make it seem a human voice came from it. What did his kind need with the functions humans had? It was so primitive when thoughts could be passed without a word. Food, as humans called it, was not necessary, and even this tedious walking was an annoyance when they usually glided

256

wherever they wanted to go without any trouble.

This Earth was a pleasant place, yet for so long they had watched humans destroying it. But now was the reckoning, now was The End.

One more of their days to go and the Earth would be free of the human race forever. A pity about the other beings here but man had been killing them for years, some creatures had gone forever, and the rest would go too unless they could adapt.

How strange to be here after watching them for so long, to behave as a human (in some ways), to know that soon it would all change. The time could not come quickly enough, he and his kind would soon discard this human shape, they would call the Earth 'Acapia', after their own planet, a planet that had been in trouble for some time due to its changed orbit and close proximity to other planets. But this planet Earth was distant from those causing pressure on Acapia, and would be a good place to live when it had been cleansed of humans.

He passed a church, words came drifting through the open door as the congregation sang "He who would valiant be, against all disaster". Well, tomorrow the disaster would arrive! What pitiful language, how easy it had been for the Acapians with their superior intelligence to learn.

As the day wore on he saw some of his own walking among the humans but they did not acknowledge each other, soon enough for that after The End.

The next day was as bright as the Sunday had been, they had all assembled early, not in large crowds but in small groups, having realised it was not the thing to meet in crowds except for at some events. They had in the past taken advantage of football matches, race meetings, seaside outings, and all the strange places people would congregate, and had managed to pass on information in those places without drawing attention to themselves.

Today it had been a disused airfield with empty hangars, the cover story was ready for anyone who came asking, "We are investors, we heard it was for sale? We would like to reopen the airfield for commercial travel." Yes, it was all prepared, yet not needed for no one came to enquire; only their own came.

There had been some problems until they realised that all humans did not do exactly the same things in different parts of the planet. But they were now familiar with the different cultures, and no one anywhere suspected they were not human, and The End was near. At last the forces of Acapia could set into motion all they had planned, for today was the day.

Monday was still clear and sunny when they and all their own kind in so many countries left the last meetings, it was 10 a.m. in this country. Soon the clouds began to gather, people began muttering about the weather forecast being wrong again. It got darker, by eleven it was barely half light, thunder and lightning were expected, but none came. Some people were getting alarmed at the unusual colours appearing in the darkening sky, there was talk of a chemical accident, or of another country over the water 'sending' this phenomenon, of a possible eclipse. Many people had already rung their local radio stations to ask if a full eclipse was expected, and if not, why it was dark for so long. No answers could be given. There was panic on news and weather stations everywhere.

All the world leaders were frantically phoning to see if their enemies, or 'friends' in other countries knew what was happening.

No country was omitted from the darkness; the entire human race was enveloped in the same unexplained dusk. As it became darker, panic began to grip people, they huddled together looking fearfully upwards, but no storm broke, there was no thunder or lightning in the skies, just a strange stillness everywhere. People poured out of buildings into the streets, school teachers debated whether it was safer to keep the children in school or send them home.

Across the great oceans, even where it was night an eerie stillness disturbed and frightened people, they got up to gaze from their windows and to wonder what was wrong.

It began to get even darker, radio stations were jammed with calls for information, local councils and governments were in turmoil. Soon it was black all over the Earth, all lighting had failed, no radio, television, telephone, nothing on Earth was working, all became still.

Slowly it became lighter, people were standing, sitting, lying, wherever they had been, they had remained as if frozen. The sky was full of machines, great oval devices shining against the now blue sky, all waiting. So it was in China, India, America, above every country on Earth, the machines waited.

Slowly at first the people moved, but they did not move of their own accord. They rose directly in the air from where they were. Those in buildings or cars simply glided out of windows or doors that opened for them, and they too rose straight up in the air. It was as if they were hypnotized, silently into the ships in the sky they glided. After a short time some of the craft departed at great speed.

Where were they going? To the planet Acapia—the only place suited for human life. Now the planet Earth would soon be free of fighting, there would be no more abusing the planet, and the Acapians would have a safe place to be at last.

Acapia was different to Earth, but it was almost at the end of its cycle of life, so let the humans have it, they would not be there for long.

More and more of the Acapians gathered as the day wore on, watching their craft take aboard the humans and leave. They were eager to clear the human debris left behind—cars trains, buildings—and leave only the things that nature had produced here.

So all towns, cities and villages became empty, the Acapians gathered in deserts, countryside, plains, open areas everywhere. Soon there were no mortals left at all, the space craft had all gone and the humans with them. The End for human life on Earth was now.

Slowly the new dwellers of Earth set about removing the evidence that human life had been there at all. No demolition gangs were needed for the demolishing of buildings, just the deadly rays from the centre of their craft, leaving nothing, not even a pile of rubble behind. Methodically the Earth was cleared until no traces remained of what had been there until only a short time ago.

So now the day was Wednesday and the Earth was still, no children's laughter, no cars, no airplanes, and no sounds that humans make at all. Only the gentle gliding of the Acapians as they moved around from area to area.

The Earth was tranquil, each country empty of life, though some animals still existed, having awakened from the hypnotic spell of the Acapians they wandered freely, it was now their planet, theirs and that of the new residents. The Acapians were putting into effect many changes, strange shapes began to appear where once buildings had stood, oval in shape, long shimmering dwelling places.

On the second week when all the mortals were no more, fleets of space craft began landing, silently and swiftly. From these came the rest of the Acapians, bringing what they considered necessary and leaving anything that was useless behind on Acapia for the humans.

The Acapians were unlike humans in form, being oval in shape with round heads, and small pieces on the end of the body which they glided upon, and small extensions half way down the body which moved. The head had a slit in the front from which came deadly rays that could destroy quietly. A smaller slit further down the head was the only other break in the perfect outline of the Acapians.

The new planet was theirs, all their own kind had now arrived, much work had been done and it was as they wanted it. The remaining animals were content; they had their food which the Acapians did not need and had no fear of the new residents.

A new way began on Earth; the long oval shapes on the ground became busy places, places of thought and learning. All their previous study of the Earth and its inhabitants had been worthwhile, the ability to alter their own shape, knowledge of weather patterns and nature, all was in the Acapians favour. These were intelligent beings far beyond the human capacity and they had used that intelligence to take care of their own.

So the years went by, who knows what had become of

262

human life? Had it all perished? There was air on Acapia to breathe but not the rich resources of Earth. Acapia had not been expected to survive for long, had it disappeared taking the mortals with it? Or had some of the more enterprising humans—once they had recovered from the trance they had been placed in— tried to save mankind?

On Earth, all was well, even more advancement had been made and the animals had realised that if they left the new residents alone, they would be left alone and were content.

The Acapians were settled, they were growing in numbers, the ease of reproducing new beings of their advanced intelligence did not inconvenience at all. It was simple to pass on the thought that more Acapians were needed, and within two thought transferences new beings would emerge from one of the long oval shapes on the ground. Nothing was hard, it all was incredibly easy, almost too easy, and those in charge of this new world saw nothing ever stopping this existence.

But light years away from Earth, the planet Calliton had sent travellers to view Earth in their craft; their planet was having problems too. They were running out of the things they needed for life, water, food, the air was becoming heavy, food would not grow without water, no seas remained on the planet, it was becoming a wasteland. They had sent craft all over the universe searching for a new home, and the planet Earth seemed to have all they required.

So it was decided that these beings with the long bodies, a round head that had two openings at the top in the front, had to go. So the first craft set out to infiltrate, sure that they could mingle, change shape, become as the beings on Earth were. The intelligence of the Earth creatures was far below their own, the planet of Calliton was failing, it would be the end for them if they did not go soon.

The unused green fields, the water, the clean air, this was what was needed, the beings inhabiting the Earth did not need it, and for them it would be The End.

So began another cycle of change on Earth as the Callitons mixed with the Acapians, and their plans took shape. For the Earth dwellers the final day was coming and a new race would soon become the new inhabitants in their place, in effect, The End.

The End

About the Author

I hope you enjoyed this compilation of Jessie's short stories. Jessie also wrote children's stories and poetry. Jessie had a lifelong love of nature which is very clear in her poetry, and both a vivid imagination and a cheeky sense of humour which is evident in her short stories.

Though Jessie grew up in Nottinghamshire and travelled extensively, her true home was the Isle of Wight where she lived for twenty-five years.

Jessie is also the author of The Complete Poetry Collection of Jessie Booth and The Adventures of Ulona the Unicorn. You can find out more about Jessie's work by visiting her blog at: http://jessiespoetrypage.blogspot.com

Printed in Great Britain
by Amazon